T0354767

He Will Exist

Margaritë Camaj

Cover Illustrated by: Gjystina Lumaj

authorHOUSE®

AuthorHouse™
1663 Liberty Drive
Bloomington, IN 47403
www.authorhouse.com
Phone: 1 (800) 839-8640

Published by AuthorHouse 7/21/2015

ISBN: 978-1-5049-2294-4 (sc)
ISBN: 978-1-5049-2295-1 (e)

Library of Congress Control Number: 2015911268

In loving memory of

**Martin Camaj
Christina Marie Barone
Marielle Bancou-Segal**

This comes from my soul...

I wanted to, first and foremost, thank God for giving me my soul and the consistent power and will to write.

I want to thank my Mother who has been my number one emotional supporter when I had no one else to turn to. She knew what to do to make me feel okay. Few had the power to do that. I thank her for always showing me the importance of good work ethic. You not only believed in me, Mama, but you understood me. That was rare.

I also want to thank my Father for always allowing me to be free with my soul and for not trying to change who I was at the core. He taught me to love my culture, but he also taught me to not be confined by it. He taught me to never forget where I came from no matter where I go.

Then, I want to thank those few who have steadied my hand and helped me remain focused even when my faith was shaken. You all hold a special place in my heart. The few of you know who you all are.

Lastly, I want to give a special thank you to those who told me that I wouldn't amount to nothing in my childhood and in some of my darkest days throughout my life. It made me the strong independent woman that I am today and it pushed me to complete this book. I want to personally thank you, from the bottom of my soul, for doubting me.

In Loving Memory of *Martin Camaj*,

When you see the [M.C.] initials, know that they do not just stand for Margaritë Camaj. Instead, I hold another soul that is deeply intertwined in mine. That soul is my own brother, who has instilled his spirit in me, even though he is not present with us today.

Because of this, my strength has always been doubled. His divine force has given me the gift of possessing what I call an "un-killable soul." I need to explain this though. I have been able to overcome any fear and obstacle that has been thrown my way no matter how difficult it might have seemed at first. I call this my God-given gift. He is my blessing.

In Loving Memory of *Christina Marie Barone*,

You taught me what loss was when I was only a teenager. You also taught me that people may leave, some due to God's necessity, but their soul will live through yours forever.

In Loving Memory of *Marielle Bancou-Segal*,

You showed me what it felt like for someone to never doubt in me. You blessed me with knowledge of the value of the arts. You gave me the chance to make Fire Island my soul's home.

You can get through anything...

There were times when I felt so alone that the only way I could connect with anything was with a pen in my hand. I allowed my heart, mind, body, and soul to spill onto paper. This was the only way I would feel complete freedom. I felt as if I could spill everything out to it. I wasn't judged. I wasn't restricted. I felt unconditional love. See, I had a fear of people leaving my life and I was sure that the pen and paper were stable. They would always be there.

This book is dedicated to all those who have felt alone, even though you have others who love you and have loved you to the best of their ability. There are just some things that you have to go through alone because, sometimes, nothing anyone else says will help. You have to help yourself.

Know that there is hope. Know that there is a light in the darkness. Know that nothing is empty. Know that we are here for a purpose. There has to be something greater than our limited years on earth. Whether you believe in God or not, no matter what religion you are, no matter what race you are, no matter how society defines you, I beg you all to dig deep inside of your bodies and dig your souls out. You have to do this in order to connect with your emotions because we are humans and there are many times that we forget we truly are raw: without all the excess.

Allow your heart to lead your path and do not allow your mind to be the sole thing that consumes you. Do not allow yourself to forget what your heart contains. This is peace. This is happiness. This is what happens when you allow your heart to swallow your mind. You become free.

This book was my healing. It helped me come closer to peace.
This is what I used to heal myself. But words of others
have helped tremendously as well. I hope that these
words will aid in your healing process.

How I wrote my letters:

As is true with people who are in touch with their artistic side, my writing is what keeps me sane in a world that consumes us at times. I wrote a majority of these letters while I was in law school.

I knew no other escape except for my writings. I didn't care to follow the crowd nor did I care to socialize very much. I mean, don't get me wrong, I had a few people that I loved to be around. However, I felt like my time was being wasted when I was around others who I felt that I could not trust or that I could not build with. So, I would have rather been alone with my pen and paper. It was my stability. I needed this escape so I could tap into the creative side of my mind every once in a while, especially since law school was so structured and pressure filled. This was a part of me that I kept hidden because I feared that others entry into my mind would make me vulnerable. There was no other better way to dig deep into my emotions, a part that was rarely touched in school, other than to write.

Caution: Sometimes the mind creates things that are not there. The mind sees potential. There is a great percent of the mind that we don't know. The mind is scary. It can imprison you or it can free you. Who knows? These letters are fiction, but they contain a true message. They contain real emotions intertwined with what my mind has created. When it comes down to it, these letters are something that I cannot even explain for you. I guess you all have to read them and figure it out for yourselves. After all, who am I to try to control your minds?

Blessings...

HE WILL EXIST

...I swear.

Author's Note

Understand that I am human and that I fall—a lot. Love has caused me pain, but it has also healed me every single time.

August

I just felt too much. It was as if my soul had lived for nothing except raw emotion: his raw emotion mixed with mine. It was as if nothing else mattered except for him. With him, I was starving for a truth that was nonexistent in this world. It might have been a fantasy for them, but for me, it was all I had known. It was all that I had ever wanted to know. It was all that I could know. There were times when my thoughts of him were my only reality.

He was my only calm. He was able to do that for me. I think the best thing was that he gave me hope in a time of despair. He was my only saving grace in a period when I was stuck in tragedy, and it was a tragedy that I could have even created myself. I don't know yet. But I know this: it is not even that I won't forget everything. It is not that I won't allow myself to forget him. It is something intrinsic. It lives inside of me. It is so out of my control that I cannot forget it. It is impossible. He is engrained in me.

He is a part of me. They can try, but it has reached the point where he has entered my soul. At some point and time, the universe has secretly planned every lover who has ever lived to love unconditionally and securely placed them in each other's souls. It was as if God had written it. Him without I was inconceivable. It didn't make sense. I don't know how I made it through time before, but now that I know him, he will never escape my pores.

My heart has trapped his heart inside of mine.

Now, I beg you all to listen to me even if I get a little too intense at times. Usually, people leave, and few have the strength to actually deal with my mind. I appreciate those who try, but few can ever get to the finish line. I am unsure if I am even able to get to the finish line, let alone anyone else. But, as usual, I believe in others more than I believe in myself. It has taken me a while to even get up to this point.

I think I have figured out who I am. Keyword: think. I struggled with my weight a lot. I went up and down. Sometimes, I was skinny and sometimes I wasn't. No, I wasn't "fat" or whatever you called it, but I wasn't what "they" expected. Who cares right? Because I definitely did not.

I didn't care about material things, that much, I mean, unless it was a love letter. I loved poems. I craved them. I had a sick obsession with love letters and black roses. To me, black roses had life. They represented ugliness at first, but that is the beauty of them because it is all about perception. It is all about what a human can see instead of what actually is. Like I said before, everything is created in the mind. I found beauty in a black rose because I had to dig deeper in order to discover its truth. The beauty was to be discovered later. It was hidden just like the soul.

Anyway, back to where I was going. Other than that, I could not care less of what they thought about my appearance. I guess I always knew that the guy, who loved me, would fall in love with me—at least that is what I had always hoped for.

I am insecure. Of course. I would never deny that. I mean, what girl isn't? They say I'm beautiful, but like, how the hell do they know? See, the way I view beauty is something else. I can't just look at someone and call him or her beautiful. I have to know the soul. HAVE TO. And they don't know my soul. At least a majority does not.

Daily conversations are so dull, consisting of, "Hey, how are you?" This was always such dry conversation to me. I want to know who you are and all about your substance. Why are you happy? What makes you cry? What makes you feel? What makes you numb? What is the essence that you are made of? Listen, this is exactly what I mean. Few want to actually go deep into your soul. So, they can't call me beautiful because my soul has been through many wars and until they know my essence, they are incapable of making that judgment. I guess that was why I kept to myself a majority of the time.

It has always struck me so strange that we analyze atoms with a microscope in science, but we pass by humans daily without knowing the main organ that keeps them alive: their heart. We don't know the main organ that allows them to function and think: their mind. Depressing.

And yeah, I know what you're thinking. You think that I am some hopeless romantic who lives in fantasy and ignores reality. It is whatever though. I know that I am stubborn.

So, I just sit back and convince myself otherwise. It is working so far. I feed all this crazy information into my thoughts. I know it is poison, but I like the thrill. Entering my head would probably kill anyone weak—but beside the point—my head is toxic. I know one thing though. I am sure of it. I'll prove them wrong.

My escape...

Whenever I was down, Fire Island was my escape into another world. There, my soul was free. And Mama, she let me find myself whenever I needed to. Mama worried too much, but I was also a little too selfish. I was a little too consumed with myself to even care about what Mama saw. And she definitely saw. She knew everything because she loved me unconditionally, even when I doubted what the word love even meant. Mama asked, "Are you staying longer?" "Come in and eat Zemer!" Zemer means "my heart" in the Albanian language.

She didn't dare ask me what I was thinking. She was too scared to. She knew my thoughts could do some serious damage. She didn't want my thoughts to cause an earthquake in my body, slowly trembling all of my cells. She knew that my thoughts barely even allowed me to sleep during the night.

"MA!" I snapped. Mama asked, "Are you okay?"

I said, "Sorry Mom, I just want to write a little more and you interrupted my writing. Now, I am all over the place!"

I raised my voice. I fucking hated myself for it. Why couldn't I be normal? I knew she loved me, but I would still snap at her pointlessly when I knew that she was just worried about me. I told her that I would come inside and eat soon. She wanted a kiss on the cheek, but I was so unemotional. I didn't even know how I got to be this way. I had become a cement wall even though my insides were too emotional. I was a contradiction.

But, as always, I felt bad for snapping. I jumped up and gave her a kiss on the cheek. I also smiled one of my big fake smiles.

Mom said, "You're just like your dad. You love so deeply and you have such a good heart, but it is hard for you to show your emotions…"

I heard her voice fading as she probably walked away. I looked at the water, and I was lost again. Of course I didn't notice that she left. I didn't notice anything. I disappeared into my own zone, just like I always did. He was there, somewhere.

That was how my days and nights went by in Fire Island.

Letters to Him, 1,

I dove into the deep blue sea as I closed my eyes and thought of chaos. Do I want to swim back up and recapture a new breath of fresh air or should I continue to place a strong pressure on my mind state?

My heart spoke so loud that my mind did not even hear its thoughts as the waves kept crashing down on them, perfectly silencing them while my heart continued to pound loudly. I could not hear my thoughts. They were drowning me. I was told that the water was supposed to give me new life, something quite similar to rebirth, but I just did not believe it until his soul, that resembled mine, lent out his hand.

It was at that moment that I understood that I had to slowly pick myself apart from the disorder of the high tide, in which my body was submerged, and attempt to grasp that bit of fresh air. It was the only thing that could save me from drowning. I needed it. He did it.

I was convinced that he was the male version of me. I was saved.

[M.C.]
August 16, 2013
4:33PM

I stared back at the waves and I closed my eyes. I felt a little relief. Every single time I wrote to him, I felt as if I were letting something out of my chest: a soft gasp. It was as if, I were communicating with him. He always healed me. Writing healed me. Both were my saviors, indirectly.

Letters to Him, 2,

I have decided to let you save me. The key was to let my heart swallow my mind. I did not listen to what anyone said about you. Not a soul could change me. I did not want to worry about anything else except making the heart happy because I didn't do that last time. I failed. You see, if we are committed, we end up with the person we love.

That person has to complete us and make us better. We are the ones who take all the responsibility and all the consequences. Society just doesn't. So, why listen?

I wish I could yell at the top of my lungs: "SOCIETY: JUST LET US LOVE! LET US LOVE!" And I want to love, in a true way, because I didn't have that in the past. I am unsure how, but you have shown me that in such a short time. I don't want to lose my chance to have truth. I don't want to lose truth and gain society's views.

And you, I hope you don't judge me. I hope you will be able to understand that I was put through this for a reason. My past led me here. He hurt me. He did. But, my broken heart led me here. It led me to you.

[M.C.]
August 16, 2013
5:00PM

I looked at my phone: 7 missed calls. Of course. They were all from Mama. I had forgotten to go inside and eat. I had become so irresponsible when it came to my parents. I gathered all of my stuff and ran to the house. I quickly wiped away my tears and smiled the whole way home. I did not want Mama and Pops to know that I wrote again.

My words were so real that they brought me to tears many times. I found myself tearing without realizing it. My writing triggered certain emotions for me.

Mama wasn't oblivious though. She knew that I was writing. And she saw these black ink marks that were not about to escape my hands any time soon. I secretly liked them though. My hands reminded me of black roses. They were beautiful tattoos, to me, at least.

Three days have passed and nothing has changed. My patterns have remained the same. Sleep is my enemy. I stay on the beach all night and I write under the moon. During the day, I am lost in the sunlight, desperately waiting for nightfall to arrive. I pick up my pen, again. It is the only thing that never fails me.

Letters to Him, 3,

Lost and found.

Those two words have flown throughout my mind in the most beautiful and most ugly ways known to mankind. But I get it. And I think he will get it, too. Although I fear, at times, he won't. I often find my thoughts contradicting themselves, just like these two words and you.

These two words, combined with the thought of you, have meant more to me than anyone else could have ever known. And, I wonder if there is an outside power who can understand me, as well. Maybe there is. Actually, I am almost certain that there is. As I sit here, on these thousands of tiny grains of sand, I try to find traces of you.

I search everywhere to try to find the ones you left, but I can't. I quickly become so lost. I jump up because I can't take these thoughts. It is all due to these fears that I have. It comes from my fear of abandonment and the fear of you leaving even though you haven't even arrived yet. I stare out into the ocean and I can't trust it, so I quickly open my eyes. Your voice haunts me.

Your absence kills me, slowly, cell by cell, wave by wave. I used to be able to trust the waves so well, but I have somehow lost myself in the ocean. My soul has drowned and I fear that it won't be found. But still, I run away, here, sometimes. It is a contradiction because I am lost and found at the same time. Here, on Fire Island, in this exact spot, I find myself again. Maybe, one day, you will too. Maybe, one day, you will understand.

[M.C.]
August 19, 2013
3:00AM

I woke up as the sun hit my eyes. They struggled to open, as always. The smell of the rusted ink on my notepad made me feel nauseous. It was probably just because I knew that I had to leave Fire Island for a bit.

I remembered that it was time to go back home, so I took one last look out to the ocean. I knew that I wouldn't return until next summer. This was my safe haven. I was so nervous. This was when my anxiety always kicked in. I didn't know what to expect for the next year. I didn't know where I would stand. I knew nothing. And, I had this sick fear of the unknown. I liked things that I could actually control, at least kind of.

All I knew was that I wouldn't have this place to escape. This was where my soul had whispered that you were the only one for me. But, until then, until my return, I promised myself that I would hold on to my writings. That was how I would remember him. My pen bled and the salt water hit my feet again, quickly, as if it removed all of my sins.

I thought that, maybe, I will have you next time because at that moment, I was drained without you here in the physical form. I was depleted. I was small. I heard myself saying, "Until, next time, Fire Island." I closed my eyes and I still did not trust the waves. Apparently, I had a tendency to love things I didn't even trust. Or maybe, I just didn't trust my own self. I didn't trust my mind. I didn't trust the unknown place Fire Island took my soul every time I was here.

September

I could have sworn that the water had kissed my mind so passionately that it had washed away the pain. Simple yet heavenly. It started off beautiful and peaceful, but it turned out to be one of the most chaotic storms that has touched my soul. I literally felt the concept of peace slowly eliminating itself from my body as the waves kept pulling me towards the depths of the waters. The life was being sucked out of me as I drowned. I tried to scream, but I was left with no voice. It had been stolen from me. Something strong was holding my lungs together so tight that I had forgotten to breathe. Everything distracted me from my breath. I couldn't see the white sand. This black fog had appeared everywhere and nothing was in sight. As I was drowning, I saw him under the water. I couldn't tell if he was dead or alive.

I woke up. I wasn't there. I was, here, in my bed. I took my right hand and put it over my heart. I didn't understand how it could beat so fast, but it was barely functioning. I wished my thoughts would just stop. They almost killed me every single time.

I had a bad habit of analyzing my dreams. I didn't know if they were dreams or nightmares, but I knew that they felt too real. Believe me when I say that there was no way out of that water. None. I didn't even want there to be a way out—so there just wasn't. You all know that I said that the mind can create anything, but my mind didn't want to create an escape. You see, no matter what my heart may want, my mind has already determined its desire. All else became irrelevant. All else became meaningless. And, I realized, that is where I fucked up.

Letters to Him, 4,

I haven't slept. The fact that I am back here, without him, has instilled this deep fear within my soul. I keep waking up with violent screams that wake up my mom and dad. They are both worried sick about me, but I really don't have anything to fear anymore. I love them and I want them to know that. It is just kind of weak. I am weak. Nothing. Never mind. I'm sure you won't get it anyway. I guess those nightmares are the only things that keep me alive. I feel nothing during the daytime. Back to reality.

[M.C.]
September 3, 2013
6:33AM

I take a deep breath as I enter class. I look around and nothing is familiar. Everything is new, just like this feeling that I have in my chest. I was always quite resistant to change. I feared it. Maybe because, in the past, nothing had really remained constant.

But, you have somehow seemed to remain the only constant thing in my mind. You have yet to escape. As the days go by, I realize that I fear things in life more and more. It feels like this big tumor keeps growing in my mind and there is no way to remove it.

I think to myself, "Am I even living?" Everywhere I go, I feel as if you are my only hope. It is because of you that hope resides somewhere inside of me. It is just so difficult to find it at times. I hope you will understand how this hurts me and how the fear of loving you breaks me into little pieces.

Letters to Him, 5,

    Why does everyone walk around so emotionless? As if they fear life, myself included. We are walking hypocrites. We talk about love all day long and we don't do anything about it. We talk about hurt, but we don't do anything about it. We talk about trust as if it is a theory that is never put into practice. Maybe we have a bigger problem. Maybe we don't trust ourselves. Maybe we see the harm that is self-inflicted. If we hurt ourselves so much, what makes us think that we could actually trust others? I wonder if time is a problem that we create. I think that is why, at times, I hate it here. We talk about love. But it is as if we, as humans, have never really existed.

[M.C.]
September 5, 2013
11:03AM

"Merzi!" The professor called on me to read a case brief out loud. I was stuck. I quickly rummaged through all of my typed papers so I could find the brief. My heart started to race. I hated being the center of attention. Even if I knew something perfectly, it was so difficult for me to speak on it out loud. It was like I had too many things inside of my head.

The professor said, "Did you do your work? If you didn't, just tell me ahead of time and I will not call on you. Next time, come prepared."

"Fuck!" I thought to myself. "This can't be good."

"I found it," I said quietly. I started reading the facts, the opinion, and the holding of the case.

"Not so bad, was it?" The professor said. "Good job."

It wasn't that I didn't know it. Of course I knew it. I've always been a pretty good student, but I just had this weird feeling that was occurring inside of me every single time I had to speak about something. I got a weird feeling inside of me whenever I really spoke about anything at all. I was quick to malfunction.

My brain functioned in class. I swear that I tried to learn, but it was so difficult for my heart to be completely in it. I concentrate solely on emotions. It is as if I have two different minds, one that works with my heart and one that doesn't. And, they both fight constantly.

It is as if my heart and my mind are two separate entities. They don't work together. My brain does its own thing and my heart is somewhere else. I zoned out again in class. I thought about how I was when I was younger. I thought about what life was like for me and where I went wrong. I was convinced that something in my childhood had to go wrong because I was so different from everyone else. They all were able to have their heart there, ready to be in full use. It was as if, they were ready to conquer anything. They were okay with blending in and socializing and I was in my own world for a majority of the time—unless I was writing to him. I closed my eyes, in class, like a weirdo, and I thought about how my life was like when I was just a child:

Seven-year-old Merzi's mind...

I am so happy. I guess being with my family makes me feel this way. My dad takes me everywhere. I mean EVERYWHERE. He is kind of like my savior. My dad reminds me of this man they talk about a lot—-God. I kind of compare daddy to him. I love them both equally. You know, I really look up to daddy. I want to be just like him when I grow up. Just like now, he picked me up from school, and brought me a book. I know it is not chocolate, or candy, but I love it just as much. He always brings me books, but this one was extra special. We don't have much money—-so, this book means so much. It is a little ripped, but that didn't matter to me. It is beautiful. The way that the sun hit the girl's face on the cover was pretty. I want to be just like her when I am older. She shines and she is set free while running into the water. She doesn't worry about a thing. She kind of reminds me of myself.

My dad promised me that if I read this book, he would take me to the Park on the dead end of Webster Avenue and 204th street in the Bronx. No one usually comes with me—only dad. I don't have any brothers or sisters. I am fine with that though because my parents always make me feel loved. This park makes me feel like I am in a completely different world even though it is on a dead end street. I don't really know why, but it is my escape. No one really comes to that park so it is never crowded. I think it is one of the gems of the Bronx. Why do I say gems? Well it is me and daddy's secret, but I'll let you in on it. He usually takes me to a place that not a lot of people know about. He always tells me that it is good to read books there. I look at the book cover and then I look at reality—-not much of a difference. I see train tracks, a little pond with water, and some rocks spread around the ground. It is perfect—just like a fairy tale. It feels like nothing can go wrong. Everything was bright and the sun was shining everywhere. I think I just fell in love with something for the first time. I don't know what love is, but I hear my parents telling me they love me and that they love the little things. So, I love the water like they love me. Does this make sense? I guess I will try to explain later. All I know is that I am really, really happy. Daddy looks at me. He tells that he is proud that I am reading. I close my eyes and say a prayer. Daddy said that this is what peace feels like. He said that this is what peace is." [M.C.] **Thoughts in 1998**

Back to reality...

I snapped out of it. My life always seemed so perfect to outsiders. I guess people never really care to look inside the heart of someone yet they are so quick to judge whatever we show on the outside. I can't live like this. I just can't. I always

knew that I was different, but I embraced that, even though, at the same time,
I hated it because I knew that he was the only one who I thought was like me.

Before I knew it, class was over. It was strange because I had five full pages of notes written down but I didn't even remember when I had the time to write them down. My thoughts wandered all the time. My subconscious had its own heart. This was tough because I had to go home and learn everything all over again.

The long drives home were my favorite part, especially during the Fall, because everything was dying. Everything was cold. I loved the cold because it mirrored my soul. "You Found Me" by The Fray came on the radio and I felt a strong sting in my heart. It started beating fast and my breath distracted my mind. I kept thinking of Fire Island and how I couldn't wait to go back. I know you will read this so I guess that this is the only thing that keeps me going. You exist, right? I had to stop and write down what I was thinking.

Letters to Him, 6,

Love always confused me. Everyone spoke about this beautiful entity that combined two people and formed them into one. But where was the proof in that? I witnessed love as being a constant violent struggle. You gave and didn't get. You tried and it wouldn't be reciprocated. You were broken down into pieces of "love" until every bit of love disappeared.

It was pretty refreshing when he walked in my life. I felt like I could take a breath of fresh air that wouldn't damage me. It wouldn't interrupt the way my insides worked. And I didn't fear that the air wouldn't be supplied anymore. He was consistent. That is love.

[M.C.]
September 16, 2013
6:33PM

On the days that I came back home from school, I wrote. I didn't know much else except for this. At night, I would look at the moon many times. It was as if my soul bled for it. It was as if it was my only way of communication. My pen brought me back to you.

There were times were the nights were the worst. The nightmares just did not stop. They haunted me. My mom and dad hated them. They knew I wasn't okay, but they didn't want to hurt me by asking me too many questions. To cure the pain, I wrote to him.

Letters to Him, 7,

My heart and smile were drained. They were drained into something I thought that I couldn't regain. It was so difficult for anyone to be able to really put a smile on my face. I tried though. I was determined to somehow pick myself up and not constantly injure my soul because my soul was all I had. He was my soul. I felt the obligation to protect him.

[M.C.]
September 21, 2013
12:31AM

Time...

I am sitting here on the sand and I am staring out into the ocean. I can feel the depth of my eyes match in color and connect in strength with the ocean water. My soul is big and while one may only see the salt and bitterness, another may attempt to find its depth. The oxygen needed to keep one alive, in order to reach the bottom, is only made for one person. I am one with the ocean. The wind that hits my face, blows my hair into the crisp atmosphere, trying to take me back in time so that I can somehow reach you once more. My soul begged you to reveal what you know so that you could save me. Sometimes, I wish the wind would blow my soul to yours so your soul and mine can form into one. I am lost here, but I like it. That is where I found you in the first place.

"Fuck." I yelled. That was a nightmare.

Letters to Him, 8,

God has a big plan for us. The beauty in His love is that He does not make us entirely dependent on Him. He makes us independent with a sense of responsibility for our actions and words. Free will is given to us in order to allow us to choose our strengths and weaknesses. He tests us in order to see what composes our loyalty to Him through how we treat people on earth. He was testing me, constantly. He wanted me to prove to myself that I was, in fact, strong enough.

I could survive anything. God knew that I could. That is why my mind is so intense. I could not only handle these thoughts, but I could do something positive with them. I wrote these letters.

[M.C.]
September 30, 2013
11:02PM

Letters to Him, 9,

You shouldn't fear losing the self when you love. Love should be a fear of losing the other person because your physical and emotional limbs don't work without the other. Love is selfless and should be a complete immersion in the other.

[M.C.]
September 30, 2013
11:59PM

Insomnia became my best friend. You see, they thought that I was awake. Technically, I was, in theory, but in practice, my soul was asleep. There was a struggle to be awake in this society. It has been proven time and time again that I was a contradiction. As time passed, I stayed up writing. The seconds turned to minutes and the minutes turned to hours. My mind could not stop even if my heart had wanted to. I kept going. I kept writing.

O_{ctober}

My love is too strong for my body. At times, it is almost unbearable and it causes me to hate the fact that I am even capable of loving at all. This is where the contradiction kicks in again. Just listen to this. At the same time, love is the only thing that keeps me alive.

It is not that I cannot be alone. It is that I hated the thought of being without you. My soul cries out to you even when I try to steal away its oxygen. I cannot do it. I never find enough air to breathe peacefully. I fear that I will never be the same. This is how I justify all of these actions that everyone finds a problem with.

They think I am hurting myself, but it is the only way that I know how to survive. I allow my soul to deplete until I feel something. I will allow you to see exactly who I am. The only way that I know how to do so is with this pen.

I woke up with nightmares a lot and, to be honest, they drained me. I would never admit it to anyone other than these letters. I had thoughts of you every night. I hated these nightmares because I loved to be in control of my mind and when I would fall asleep, it was obviously completely out of my control. This did not just happen on random nights. They were consistent. These nightmares appeared every single night. I wouldn't have wished this on my worst enemy. There goes the contradiction again. Just listen to this. I wouldn't have wished this on my worst enemy, right? But, in a way, I was my worst enemy. Funny, right? Why did I think that I could handle this, but no one else could? I didn't even know how to cure myself anymore. An outer force completely took over me. You became a disease that traveled throughout my mind, dissecting every part of me, very carefully. This disease learned every part of my body, mind, heart, and soul. It knew me better than I knew myself. You consumed me.

The Subconscious Mind...

God: *You seem destroyed.*

Merzi: *Wh—at do you mean?*

God: *You are empty. I can't really seem to figure out what emotions consume you.*

Merzi: *EMOTIONS?*

God: *Yes. You don't know what those are? Your heart is supposed to spill them out.*

Merzi: *I...I have no feeling in my heart. EVERYONE says that I am heartless.*

God: *What do you see in everyone?*

Merzi: *Are you kidding me? I see NOTHING. Actually, I fucking see something. I see hate. I see hate because THEY made me that way.*

God: *Who are "they?"*

Merzi: *"They" is EVERYONE, LITERALLY—-EVERYONE who ever took away a piece of me until I had no more pieces left.*

God: *But, I am here for you. I always was. You don't remember when you were a little girl and you put your faith in me?*

Merzi: *My faith? What is that? I lost that a long time ago. I believed in YOU. I was alone, but no one helped me. You didn't even help. I prayed to you every night, but my days kept getting darker and darker. I asked you to help me out. Actually, I didn't ask. I begged. But you didn't pull me out. You didn't lend that hand. You let me drown, just like everyone else.*

God: *I was always here. I know what is best for you. Have faith.*

God: *Answer me.*

God: *Hello.*

God: *I've been calling you for days now. Where have you gone? I need your response.*

God: *I am trying to help you...*

I woke up. Maybe I was creating Hell in a place where Heaven wanted me to thrive, but I just couldn't deal with this anymore. It was as if my whole faith had left me. I did not want to get up. I did not want to feel my body moving. I wanted to drown in myself, by myself. I did not want anyone around. I did not want to answer Him.

I knew He kept calling me, but I didn't know what to believe anymore. I felt faith slowly leaving my body. Nothing seemed okay. It wasn't even that I hated God, but I knew that I couldn't love Him fully at this point because you were not near me. You know how they say that you can't love someone else until you fully love yourself? Partially, they were right because this was why I could not love God. But, at the same time, that was complete bullshit.

I guess this was my struggle between love and hate. If I didn't quite love myself, and he was I, was it possible that I have developed a hate for him? Was it possible that I have loved him so much that it had turned to a hate for the self and a hate for him? This was really fucking scary. Hopefully, you will understand something else about me now even though you haven't even arrived yet. Do you know at least a bit of my soul at this point? Have you tasted a bit of my heart? You were great. The rest of the world was small.

The Subconscious Mind, **Letters to Him, 10,**

Conscience: Please, tell me why you are talking to him. He doesn't even care about you. He just reads about you and tries to listen to clues, but does not actually know who you are. Have you even met? Have your souls touched? Have you looked inside each other's hearts?

Merzi: (Tossing and Turning) Leave me alone. You don't know how I feel.

God: That wasn't me that said that. It was your guilty conscience. Don't fall and look at his actions before you take that step.

Merzi: Fuck!

God: Why are you always attacking me?

[M.C.]
October 19, 2013
3:00AM

Time was misconstrued. I didn't even know if I was awake or if I was asleep when I wrote this. Life seemed to either occur in my writings or in my sleep, when I had nightmares only. They were so real that they gave my life meaning. I had these nightmares that I was usually able to write about.

I woke up again.

My dream must have been from another world. God was trying to talk to me and He didn't in a long time. I almost answered, but my pride did not let me. I haven't had many conversations with God after the horrible (closes eyes) FUCK THIS, I DON'T WANT TO THINK ABOUT IT! (I swallow a deep gulp).

God frightens me. He gives me chills because I remember the purity that I had when I was one with Him. I was at peace. Now, I don't even know where God is. How could He let me be this miserable? He left me here alone. Everyone leaves…even God. All I have left are these writings to you. I drown myself in my words for long seconds, minutes, hours, days, and months. ***This was the only way that I knew how to pass time.***

November

I still write.

Letters to Him, 11,

I'm constantly reminded of God and even though I don't trust Him fully right now, somewhere deep in my subconscious, I know that God has a big plan for us. I guess that the beauty in His love is that He does not make us entirely dependent on Him. He lets us be free and make our own decisions. Maybe that is why He has not bothered to help me yet. He makes us independent with a sense of responsibility for our actions and words. Free will is given to us in order to allow us to choose our strengths and weaknesses. He tests us in order to see what composes our loyalty to Him through how we treat people on Earth. This is where I always get confused. I don't know what He is testing me with. I have not a clue. Not one. I am lost.

[M.C.]
November 1, 2013
1:52PM

I struggled to involve myself in the world. I only knew how to keep writing. I lived in my mind. I didn't allow my mind to live outside of itself.

Letters to Him, 12,

You shouldn't fear losing the self when you love. You shouldn't fear losing trust with those you love, either. I thought that love should be a fear of losing the other person because your physical and emotional limbs rarely are able to work without love. I don't know if I still believe this though. But I do know that love is selfless. I have completely immersed myself in you.

[M.C.]
November 2, 2013
11:53AM

Letters to Him, 13,

Love always confused me. Everyone had the tendency to speak about this beautiful entity that combined two people and formed them into one. But where was the proof in that? I witnessed love as being a constant violent struggle. You gave and didn't get. You tried and it wouldn't be reciprocated. You were broken down into pieces of "love" until every bit of love disappeared.

I guess it would be pretty refreshing when you walk into my life. I picture feeling like I could finally take a breath of fresh air that wouldn't damage me. You know what I mean? It wouldn't interrupt the way my insides worked. I wait for a time when I do not fear that the air wouldn't be supplied anymore. He would be consistent. That is love.

[M.C.]
November 3, 2013
11:59PM

Letters to Him, 14,

I'm starting to feel hopeless again. I feel like I might be getting into one of those traps. Fuck. The fear starts to accelerate and build throughout my body. I can't control it. It takes over me completely. And, my veins start to freeze. I love him and I know that he loves me. WAIT! I mean, I guess he does. No, I know. Fuck. Whatever. It is reversing once again. Everything that usually happens, happens. I try not to think of the negative, but how can I do that? They tell me to stop, but they don't understand how this feels. It is overpowering. It takes over me. I don't understand how someone who is apparently so sorry can act so suddenly negative towards me. Shouldn't it be enough that I am giving my all after everything that occurred? Sometimes, I feel so close to him and then he rips me into pieces without meaning to and he pulls me back again. I can't believe that he can utter these words. What words? Have we even spoken before? I don't know what I'm saying. My mind needs to fucking stop.

[M.C.]
November 4, 2013
11:59PM

Letters to Him, 15,

What the hell do I do now? Now feels so empty. There is nothing in now. Nothing at all. Not an atom defining it. Alienation from now has replaced it. It was you who taught me to slowly pick myself up when I needed it the most. I'm not sure how, but you did it. I couldn't even do it myself and then you came along. You were something that I didn't know that I ever needed. Maybe because I didn't need you. Maybe that is why I didn't know. What the fuck are you saying, Merzi? "Shut the fuck up." My mind doesn't let me think for myself. It controls me sometimes. Anyway, back to what I was saying. I didn't want it that's for sure, but I inhaled you. You gave me oxygen. The oxygen that I needed to pick myself up and redirect my dead soul. You gave me that and I was forever thankful. But now, I'm just confused. I don't fucking exist. I mean you don't exist. I mean we don't exist. We are one right? But you haven't even arrived yet. "Merzi shut up." There my mind goes again. Are you happy now? You gave me an illusion. I gave myself an illusion. No, you did. That is all you did for me. You made me believe it would be okay. You should have just let me drown. That way, I would have picked myself up once and then not have to fall again. Why the fuck did you do this? Did this give you some kind of sick, twisted pleasure?

[M.C.]
November 5, 2013
1:52PM

"Merzi, seriously, stop lying to yourself: you know you love him." I'm talking to myself. They all think that I have gone insane. Here I go again, trying to convince myself of different things. It is just because I don't know what to believe anymore. I'm convinced he is the other half of me. Then, at times, I think he shouldn't have even entered my soul. I just don't fucking get it. I can't believe I let myself love again. I swore I would never do it again.

Breathe, Merzi, it will be okay. I always had a pen and paper in my hand. When I didn't, I got this terrible anxiety inside of me. I didn't know how to let it out, so I wrote. Forgive me, everyone I love, for I had to do this. I had to rid myself of everyone to understand myself better. To understand him better.

Letters to Him, 16,

I am fully capable of falling in love with someone's mind and soul despite their physical appearance.

But they say "impossible" and "prove it".

I stop to think and only one explanation came to mind. I tell them that I have this unexplainable love and passion for God even though I have never met Him. Even though God has not arrived through my vision, He has arrived in my soul. Just like him. His soul and mind somehow spoke to me and I wouldn't care if he was skinny, fat, tall, short, handicap, or monster-like. All I know is that I love Him. He exists…well, in my mind.

[M.C.]
November 6, 2013
2:03PM

Letters to Him, 17,

    She struggled a lot with love because she loved things that resembled her own soul. Everything had a dead end. She loved everything until she got too close and attached to it. Then, they would leave. Even her writing escaped her at times. She didn't know permanent because she loved things like her soul, temporary and fragile. Things that left. She loved things that resembled herself. And she didn't even love herself.

[M.C.]
November 7, 2013
9:03PM

Letters to Him, 18,

It is so hard for me to explain as I sit here in isolation. I wanted nothing more than to have you by my side. Nothing. I wanted you as bad as I had wanted the moon during the day: close yet so distant. You were supposed to be here, by my side, watching the waves roll in and out, stealing lovers' souls throughout the world. Everyone saw the same moon and I wonder if you are somewhere, too, witnessing how lonely the moon looks, just like I am doing right now. It is a full moon tonight. I bet no other eyes are sadder than mine on this night. I sit here, thinking of you and how you use to make everything okay, under this same moon. But, sadly, there is always a "but." It has aged, and so have you and I. I fear that we will never look at the moon the same way that we did that night---similar to how I fear that I will never look at you with the same set of eyes as I did that night. I have loved you stronger than the power of nature combined together. Nothing could explain it. I have loved you stronger than the moon had loved the night, that it reappeared every night, breathing nothing but consistency and certainty. But you, you felt different.

[M.C.]
November 8, 2013
11:43PM

I looked around me. Everything was starting to change. I didn't feel anything. I didn't want to talk to anyone. I wanted isolation. I craved hate because love had overwhelmed me. But, somehow, I still couldn't be that selfish. I still looked after those who I loved even though they didn't think that I did. I wanted to keep them safe because I knew well what it felt like to feel unprotected.

Letters to Him, 19,

Have you ever witnessed the soul of a younger you in another person's body? I'm talking about a striking similarity, so intense, that you start to feel a lump in your throat. Your heart starts beating faster and faster and you feel this rush of coldness throughout your body. Suddenly, you've become a paralytic. Thoughts start coming to your mind as you stare at this little girl and analyze her every move. Although there is evil in the room, her smile eliminates it all. She dances freely as your thoughts get dizzy. This girl was the younger you, wasn't she? She has your soul now. I guess the paralysis was caused by the fear you have for her. You were full of life, too, but way before all of this happened. You saw everyone as a blessing, the good, but that diminished. You fear that ending up to be her. I was determined to protect her.

[M.C.]
November 9, 2013
3:03PM

I barely slept, like I told you before. And when I did, I was restless. My body never rested. My soul never rested. My mind never rested. My heart never rested. I was always awake, even when I was asleep.

Letters to Him, 20,

Waves.

I always craved the ocean. The colors mesmerized me. He always said I was like the ocean and that he couldn't look at it without thinking of me. He said it resembled the coldness that he felt when he tested the water out. He always had a quick reaction to remove his hand because it was too cold. However, with time, you got me to it and when you exited the water, it was even colder then entering. He always compared me to the water and I never quite understood why. Now that I'm unsure where he is, I know what he meant. He was trying to compare me to the waves and the way they would constantly come and constantly go. I'll be waiting here at the shore for you, I felt him say. He was scared that I would leave again. But he failed to realize that my soul lived in Fire Island… My soul stayed on the grainy sand, waiting for his return even though I wasn't there. Even though he wasn't there.

[M.C.]
November 10, 2013
10:03PM

NO! I woke up. I was drenched in sweat. Fire Island kept coming back to me in my nightmares. I realized it was only November. Fire Island was so far away. You were so far away. I grabbed my pen and my paper. I continued to write. I was so stupid for falling asleep. I knew what would happen when I slept. I was restless. I was never at peace. Sleeping disrupted my soul. I waited for 3 am. I always did this because, then, I would be too tired to have any nightmares.

Letters to Him, 21,

My mind is cold,
Yet, my heart burns with desire.
Some choose ice & some choose fire…

[M.C.]
November 11, 2013
1:03PM

Letters to Him, 22,

I want the light, but the moonlight won't part.
Therefore, only the darkness has my heart.

[M.C.]
November 14, 2013
3:00AM

Letters to Him, 23,

They say opposites attract.
Yet my mind and heart are opposites
And they battle, day by day, consistently.

[M.C.]
November 14, 2013
3:00PM

Letters to Him, 24,

I do not know God through sight or through touch.
He is transparent.
I know Him through the unknown.
And I've discovered unconditional love in the unknown.
Like I have for you.

[M.C.]
November 15, 2013
11:23PM

Letters to Him, 25,

I sit here,
Patiently waiting for you.
Everyone around me is happy.
I guess, at moments, I experience that happiness as well.
But, does it really count?
It is temporary because, suddenly, it comes rushing to me all at once.
And it hits me hard. It hits me like a wall of bricks.
You're invisible, but I feel you here.
I miss you. "Merzi, shut up."

[M.C.]
November 16, 2013
10:04PM

The human is the most complex. I keep writing as if I know something. I keep writing as if I know myself. I keep writing as if I know you. I keep writing as if I know the world around me. But, in reality, I know nothing. At times, I do not even understand myself yet I try to understand you. I try to understand the whole world.

To understand the human, you have to be willing to take the time to undress each layer of their skin and get into the depth of his or her core. I don't think I even do that to myself. I keep trying to find my soul, but it always escapes me. Every single time I try to grab it, it escapes from my very own hands. So, how can I expect others to stay when I run away from my own self?

I have to discover myself in order to discover love, and to discover love, one must dig through the lies, the hurt, the scars, the betrayal, and find the other's soul. Then, they must hold on to it and not let it go.

You have done that to me. Thank you.

Letters to Him, 26,

I remember every little detail even the ones you wouldn't think that I would even know. I think that is what hurts the most: the fact that I remember instead of forgetting. My memory always had this advantage over me. The mind played with my soul to the point where it almost killed it. It made my soul suffer.
I remember, I do.
I remember when I fell, emotionally.
I remember you, somehow, even though you're not here. "Merzi. He was never here." No. NO! NO! Do you see this? My mind keeps trying to suffocate me. It confuses me.
I'm lying down on my bed and I'm thinking. I think too much. I know.
But what shatters my soul is that I am starting to doubt if you ever even cared. If you ever existed.

I remember. I keep repeating this to myself. I remember.

[M.C.]
November 17, 2013
11:57PM

Letters to Him, 27,

I wait every night,
Until the time is 3:03 AM,
For that is the time that turns my certainty into doubts and my convictions
into uncertainty.
I guess you're the only one who will know what that means to me...

[M.C.]
November 18, 2013
3:03AM

Letters to Him, 28,

I have to let him go.

I keep holding on to him and I can't let go.

"Merzi, what the fuck are you talking about?"

Here I go again. I keep thinking about all of this stuff that has not arrived yet.

But I have to tell him that he is young in age and in soul.

And I'm old, not in age, but in soul.

So I have to let him go.

Forgive me...

[M.C.]
November 19, 2013
2:03PM

"Who did you even write that for Merzi?" I asked myself this over and over again. I am convinced that I knew but then again, if I really thought about it, I didn't even know how to answer it. I just wrote about whatever came to me. I wrote about whoever came to mind. "No. It was about him." There goes my mind again. That is it. I made my mind up. It cannot control me anymore. I was lying to myself. My mind always found a way to deceive my heart. I just repeated myself. I was convinced that I was crazy. I had the tendency to repeat things over and over again. Maybe I did this because it would never sink in. The mind is a funny thing. It tries to make you understand things that it already understands. But, still, you can't accept it. Strange.

Letters to Him, 29,

I have to write to you once again.
Tonight is especially hard because I'm scarred.
All of these open wounds will not recover in time to heal me.
Not until you help me patch them.
No one else has the ability to heal me, not one single soul.
Tonight hit me hard.
Haunt me! I'm scarred.

Reminiscing....

[M.C.]
November 20, 2013
10:03PM

Letters to Him, 30,

My whole heart hates you.

No it doesn't.

Haunt me! I yell.

Do anything, torture my mind and capture every part of my soul until I have no more spirituality left in me.

Do all, just do not escape from my mind!

At times, I struggle, because I always forget you.

But, my heart reminds my mind that it would be the wrong thing to do.

But, still, I hate you.

Until I tell myself, "Stop lying to yourself."

`[M.C.]
November 21, 2013
3:00AM

Letters to Him, 31,

But, I like pain because sometimes, it reminds me of you.

Tonight, it is all I have when it comes to you.

Tonight feels like my last strand of you, but what do I know? I know nothing.

There goes the contradiction again. My mind controls me yet I know nothing.

How is this possible? I am a slave to my mind yet it does not help me grow. I never made any sense.

[M.C.]
November 22, 2013
4:04AM

There were times when I beautified pain. Sometimes, when something is all you know, you can make the worst thing look pretty, too.

Letters to Him, 32,

Him & I,

   We loved pain a little too much. We loved everything a little too much because we felt too much. But, I don't necessarily think that this was bad. I think it did us good. Perhaps we loved pain because it was the only time we were actually able to feel something. It was our reminder that we were human.

[M.C.]
November 23, 2013
7:03AM

Letters to Him, 33,

I know that I loved his soul even more than he did. I wanted him to constantly better himself even more than he did. I wanted him to constantly grow. Do not be mistaken. I did not want him to change for me. But for himself. This is what love is.

[M.C.]
November 24, 2013
9:01PM

I think it was the way that I breathed. It was always a little too heavy. It was as if the world was too much for me. It was almost as if I had been carrying cement walls inside of myself for years. It was as if the urban world lived inside of her.

New York City lived inside of me and I had the burden of carrying it. But it was graceful, when I walked, peacefully, towards the water. Everyone knew I was still. It was as if I took a break from everything and my mind was at ease.

They didn't dare bother me. They let me be in peace. I was forever thankful for that, truly. So, I went by random bridges to get this feeling often. I needed this fix in order to go on.

There were times when I had to actually interact. I want you to know this. There were times when I went out with my friends, but still, I felt as if I was alone. There goes my contradiction again. It always felt like you were with me. So, how was I alone? I couldn't answer that.

All I knew was that it felt as if no matter what I did, my mind was against me. I thought too much. I wanted to figure everything out. I lived for this.

As I stared into the crowd, I experienced everything, but I experienced it so differently. I heard noise, saw people dancing, and I saw that everyone was having a good time. But, I couldn't help but stop to think of our conversations. My mind started confusing me again. "What conversations Merzi? You never even spoke to this person." But, I was a pro at blocking things out when I had wanted to, so that was exactly what I did.

I would be lying if I said that I didn't enjoy feeling this way. I never understood why I got so much pleasure from pain, but at the same time, I couldn't help but think if they all had pain. I thought that it was possible that they were just good at burying it instead of them instead of letting it out. There goes my contradiction again.

I didn't show others my pain. Instead, I spilled my pain through this ink. I looked back at the crowd and, ironically, they resembled puppets to me. I guess I couldn't judge. I hated judging anyone because I knew exactly how it felt to be judged. Still, I never cared much about what they said. I guess this leaves me to conclude that we are all puppets to something. I am a puppet to my mind.

It is like my mind controls me on a string and I cannot control it. All of this contradiction is too much for me to handle at times. I am full of it.

At the same time, I am a different kind of puppet. Most of them move around acting as if they have a purpose. Most enjoy nights at clubs and bars because they run away from their problems. I am a puppet too, but I am advantaged because I have these writings to you and I stand confirmed that there is a world bigger than this...

Until we meet again... Here goes my mind again, confusing me. "We have met. No, we haven't." I am unsure, honestly.

Letters to Him, 34,

It is on nights like these,
that I wish I had you here.
I think that they are lost and that I am found, but again, I find confusion
between these two words. There are times, like tonight, where I feel so lost
and unprotected. I feel like I am finding myself more and more everyday yet
I am losing you when you haven't even arrived yet. This is all crazy. I will find
a way to heal myself but I know you are missing. There are times when I wish
I had your arms around me to make me feel safe and loved.
I'm lost without you,
And I feel alone in a world so cold... You exist. I am sure you exist.

Tears fall....

[M.C.]
November 25, 2013
3:03AM

There were never days where I skipped writing letters. There were just some things that I have ripped up because I did not want you to ever read them. I didn't even want to re-read them myself. In those, I have denied you many times.

December

It was as if he was speaking through me at times. It was as if I knew what he was thinking even though I never even fully met him yet. I cringed every time I spoke to myself like this because deep in my soul I knew that I knew him yet my mind kept trying to convince me otherwise.

I got lost for a second and I wrote this down: **They asked him what imperfection was. He said that it was driving through the dark in a warm winter night with the windows down watching her hair blow all over the place while she was in deep thought. It was watching her slowly crumble her past struggles and break down the walls that she had built. It was the fact that any normal human soul would think we are opposites because she drank tea and I had coffee. She sought purity and I praised substances that harmed the body and soul. But we had a strong similarity: both of our minds connected. I love watching her drink tea on nights like this while she analyzes all the lyrics that make her soul happy. Music made her smile because it spoke to her. She loved the words, specifically, because she never cared much for the beat. I wasn't going to let her go. She was my heaven when all I have known in this life was hell.**

That came to me just like that. It was as if an outer power instilled it in me. It was as if he had written a letter to me through my soul. **My mind was toxic. I told you.**

Letters to Him, 35,

    Before you come to me: please fall in love with your mind before you learn to understand your heart. If needed, stay up all night so that you can drown yourself in your thoughts before you can learn how to understand your own feelings. If you do the reverse, like I did, you will lose yourself like a good soul loses itself in the midst of evil.

[M.C.]
December 3, 2013
1:03AM

Letters to Him, 36,

I constantly see so many people caring about many things that are pointless. I wish I could change the love that the youth is taught. I wish I can go back and change the love that I was taught. Love should not be calculated. Often, I think that maybe you and I can make this difference. I want nothing else but love to matter. I don't give a damn about what you wear. If you can't go outside and make a strong presence with your mind, heart, spirit, and character, I find it weak. I want us to be strong.

[M.C.]
December 4, 2013
10:03AM

Letters to Him, 37,

And though I struggled with faith many times, I stand firm in my belief that, sometimes, God sends you signs and, sometimes, those signs are people. And sometimes, you have to go to places with those people in order to understand them. Those people, I call blessings.

[M.C.]
December 5, 2013
1:04PM

Letters to Him, 38,

He wasn't my soul mate. You were. You were the only one that even whispered to me, let alone spoke…

[M.C.]
December 9, 2013
2:03PM

Letters to Him, 39,

But we are human and we cannot escape hurt. Tonight, I feel it a little too much. In all ways, I know, excuse me, WE know, pain, a little too well.

Just a little too, too well.

[M.C.]
December 13, 2013
3:03AM

Letters to Him, 40,

I guess I am figuring out who I am. That, in itself, stands beautifully alone. Anything holding my hand becomes one with me. We are equal in souls, we are.

[M.C.]
December 15, 2013
4:04AM

Letters to Him, 41,

No one probably understands the meaning of this, but, I look into the water trying to learn what trust is, was, and will be. I shut my eyes so tight. I briefly remember the moments in Fire Island although I try not to. I didn't want a bit of light passing through them and gaining any sort of vision. I wanted to remember it, but then, I felt anxiety rushing through me, as always. I opened my eyes quickly. This was hard. It was draining. Everything that I enjoyed and loved was eliminating. It was hard to even trust the water. I still loved it though. I was trying to not let go and love it just like I was trying to love you. I guess that was important.

[M.C.]
December 17, 2013
4:11PM

Letters to Him, 42,

    Tonight, I feel as if my soul has run wild yet it is still the master of its own fate. Free yet self-controlled. A beautiful paradox. Yet wherever it ran, it ran to you. Was it really as free as I had thought?

[M.C.]
December 20, 2013
9:07PM

She didn't want to leave. Leaving anything scared the life out of her, literally. She ran back, trying to face her fears, but they ate her alive. He haunted my mind. He wouldn't get out. He was a prisoner of my soul. Or, was I a prisoner of my mind?

I woke up as I remembered the nightmare that I had last night. I felt as if God was trying to talk to me again, but as always, I shut Him out. I wanted to block Him out completely, but He still found ways to come back to me. I kept thinking about what He was trying to tell me. I just couldn't figure it out.

Letters to Him, 43,

But I will love you so intensely, heaven and hell will come together and make peace.

[M.C.]
December 23, 2013
9:39PM

Letters to Him, 44,

This, this right here is heaven. But that, that over there is hell.

[M.C.]
December 24, 2013
4:03PM

I had a tendency to write about heaven and hell because I only knew extremes. I guess you can call me an extremist. I tried to figure God out a lot. I knew I would never figure Him out, but I was always on the mission anyway. I always needed to understand things that I couldn't.

Letters to Him, 45,

It all comes down to what stings your heart when you are in complete isolation. What stings the pit of your core? It comes down to who will be there when you are in the middle of the ocean. That person holds power. Will they let you drown or will they be your one piece of land: to hold and protect you?

[M.C.]
December 26, 2013
5:05PM

Letters to Him, 46,

They told me that I couldn't find peace and maybe I wasn't there yet. But, I think that I was pretty close: closer than ever. I found my peace watching the sunset. I drove until I found a destination. My heart led me here. Hopefully, my heart will lead me to you, too. You are my stabilizer. The ability for someone to stabilize you in the midst of chaos is powerful.

[M.C.]
December 26, 2013
5:39PM

Letters to Him, 47,

I hope you will never take this away from me and you will understand why I do this. This, to me, was power. It was my way of fighting. I knew no other way. Daily, I found myself fighting for the heart and the mind. This is how I kept my sanity. It was my way of feeling alive even though I might have been emotionally dead. My emotions were my bullets and they fueled my pen: the greatest weapon of all.

The transition was beautiful. My pen knew me in all of my emotional states: sad, happy, depressed, numb, angry and bitter. The pen knew me better than he could ever know me. And, that angered him. But it shouldn't have because my pen even knew me better than my own self.

Little did he know, that he provided those bullets for me. He gave me the fuel. I didn't know what I had stored in me for years: but somehow, when I wrote, it all spilled out. Somehow, it all turned into a masterpiece. Everything connected.

[M.C.]
December 27, 2013
2:03PM

Letters to Him, 48,

You were infinite. Like my love for the ocean: stable, open, honest, and endless. You were the reason for my re-birth.

[M.C.]
December 28, 2013
12:23AM

Letters to Him, 49,

I am a lover, but every day, I fight to love in isolation. And you, you are a runner, and every day you fight a battle: you try not to leave. So, I turn my back. I don't want you to see the goodbye in my eyes.

[M.C.]
December 28, 2013
1:23PM

Letters to Him, 50,

And even when blur and fog attempted to cover her soul, she was never forgotten and always seen.

[M.C.]
December 29, 2013
12:03AM

Letters to Him, 51,

There are blessings everywhere yet you walk around as if the darkness is empty and has no treasure. Be brave enough to fall in love with darkness. I know I am.

[M.C.]
December 29, 2013
1:03AM

Letters to Him, 52,

The world can be terribly weak during times of despair, especially when it comes with the loss of a loved one.

Love. That word will help you get through anything, though.

[M.C.]
December 30, 2013
5:03PM

Letters to Him, 53,

My patience is running out. But then I remind myself of all the good that can come out of waiting patiently. There are days when patience feels so bitter. Then, there are the other days, where patience brings results.

[M.C.]
December 30, 2013
7:03PM

Today, as I was walking outside on this cold winter day,
I witnessed a couple arguing.
That is normal, you know, because all relationships have problems.
But, I learned something then and there.
I promised that when I met you, I wouldn't cross the line of disrespect
because that is where all begins to crumble. I am well aware.
I promise that even our arguments will end sweet.
Until next time.

Letters to Him, 54,

You taught me the most beautiful thing a human can teach another, today. You were able to know that I was crying without me shedding any tears. What a silent masterpiece.

[M.C.]
December 31, 2013
2:07AM

January

Forgive me for this month. I mean this with my entire soul.
My body shivers every time the year begins. I hope one day the
fear for January stops. I need to learn to get through this.

Letters to Him, 55,

I feel something new. It is something that I haven't felt in a while.

It was strange because I was not used to feeling this way, but it was coming back. I will admit that I was scared. I feared that it was just an illusion. There were moments where I was really happy, but then I allowed it to get stolen from me. Notice that I did not say that they stole it from me, but that I allowed it to get stolen from me. There is a difference, but I will let you figure that difference out.

"Back to what I was saying, Merzi!" I talk to myself way too much. Here my mind goes again: "Stop interrupting your train of thought!" This was coming back a little too suddenly for my taste, but it didn't really listen to me. It still crept its way back into my life. I didn't know what to do. I didn't know how to deal. It kind of felt like happiness. Honestly, I haven't even felt it in so long that I couldn't even tell you if that is really what it is.

I'm unsure exactly what you did, but I am convinced that it is magic.

[M.C.]
January 1, 2014
1:23AM

My mind has dragged me into another year. I completely forgot the timing. This was one of the times where I just realized that time was created by humans. At times, I thought it was unnecessary. I wondered what it would be like if we had lived our lives not counting time because counting time is extremely hard. It was 2014 and it hit me harder than ever just knowing that there are seconds, minutes, hours, days, months, and even years that you have still not yet arrived. Anyway, I analyzed my surroundings and I thought: Some were happy. Some were sad. Some were surprised. Some were hopeful. Some were drunk. Some were greedy. Some were sober. Some were sinful. Some were pure.

And me? I was just at a state of being calm. I was at peace with the chaos that was inside of me. I did not see a difference in the new year. But then, at the same moment, I still realized that I just felt one with the world. I felt aware. I told you that I am a contradiction. There was the proof in it again in case you did not believe me earlier. I felt like I could not blend in, but you know what? I was okay with it. I feel it deep within. It was going to be okay.

Letters to Him, 56,

Thank you.

[M.C.]
January 1, 2014
2:03AM

Letters to Him, 57,

He used to stop me. He used to tell me what I could and could not do. You know? He tried to restrict me. You were different. You always taught me that I could do anything that I set my mind to.

And that is the beautiful difference.

[M.C.]
January 3, 2014
1:23AM

Letters to Him, 58,

They all said that she resembled the sun
Yet with time, she transformed into something like the moon.
 The light illuminated when she revealed her inner secrets in the dark.

[M.C.]
January 4, 2014
2:33AM

Letters to Him, 59,

He told me that I was like a rose in the winter: rare and quite impossible to find.

I told him that he was like the moon. Many overlooked him during the daytime: but at night, his soul came alive and it whispered all of his inner secrets.

[M.C.]
January 5, 2014
3:03AM

Letters to Him, 60,

Everyone feels the storm coming. I guess because it is tangible.
I guess that I sit here and question: why don't they feel the storm of their own hearts?
Why don't they pay attention to what the little voices tell them?
Why don't they feel what their gut tells them?
And why, why, don't they listen to it?

Ignite your Goddamn senses.
All five of them.
And know that all of those that I have mentioned are a storm within themselves.

[M.C.]
January 6, 2014
5:07PM

Letters to Him, 61,

I felt his presence whenever I was a little too far. It was something unexplainable. We were each other's ghosts, and what a tragic love that was. We would always feel each other invisibly, but our bodies would never be able to meet again...

[M.C.]
January 7, 2014
300AM

Letters to Him, 62,

    I remember it as if it was yesterday. It hurt so bad that it broke my heart. I didn't even know that there was a way to further break it, but you discovered how to that night. And, what I hate most of all is how well I remember it. I remember it almost in the exact way that I remember my own name, whenever anyone asks. It is so strange how something that came so natural can feel so bad. I felt it so well that it lived inside of me, for seconds that turned to days that turned to weeks.

[M.C.]
January 8, 2014
4:24PM

Letters to Him, 63,

Winter is my favorite season.
    I love the cold.
It reminds me of your soul:
    full of emotion, yet cold and silent.

[M.C.]
January 9, 2014
3:00AM

Letters to Him, 64,

    It was the kiss of death,
placed gently on my skin.
You took my soul and every part of my being.
    But you left.
What a tragic yet peaceful white death.

[M.C.]
January 9, 2014
10:30AM

Letters to Him, 65,

She is shaken,
    but she is still.

She is chaos,
    but she is peace.

She is hell,
    but she is heaven.

She makes sense,
    ironically.

[M.C.]
January 9, 2014
3:00PM

Letters to Him, 66,

I never understood paintings.
I was never into that type of art.
Beauty that comes from the eye never resonated with me.
Maybe that is why I never cared about his beauty.
I craved the ugly mind: his thoughts, ideas, and mental movements.
Probably because my writings were pretty damn ugly too yet to me, they were beautiful.

        He reminded me of them.

[M.C.]
January 10, 2014
4:00PM

Letters to Him, 67,

He got me one black rose.
I think that anyone would have ran away,
but I stayed.
I found it powerful because that one black rose meant more to me than any
other rose that I have received, and I have received a lot.
He didn't have much, but that black rose was full of emotion.
I will never forget.

[M.C.]
January 11, 2014
3:03AM

Letters to Him, 68,

I watch the fire burn the candle into melting pieces,
    as I feel my memories of you burn away into ashes.
      They fade away, invisibly, into the air.
      Trying to hold on to them is a struggle because every time I go near the
flame, I burn.

[M.C.]
January 12, 2014
7:03PM

Letters to Him, 69,

He taught me the power of being free.
I guess that was vital in order to survive every breath that I took.
I stared at him, strikingly, in awe.
I thought to myself that we all think that we are free in this life,
but I was proven wrong.
Something probably holds a majority of us back.
We fall trapped into material possessions and false love.
Thank you for teaching me otherwise.

Spread your wings...

[M.C.]
January 13, 2014
2:01AM

Letters to Him, 70,

Looking around, everyone had this fascination with diamonds, shoes, and cars: the fancier things in life.

Sometimes, I felt as if I didn't belong.

I never really believed in any of that.

There was only one thing in which I put all my faith in: his heart.

Though intangible, it was worth more than all else.

Those materials will not follow me to the after-life,

But, I was sure that his soul would.

[M.C.]
January 14, 2014
3:00AM

Letters to Him, 71,

Isn't it beautiful to live in ruins for a while?
Ruins like chaos, disorder, and an internal battle?
You are at war with yourself.
Re-build yourself during these times.
The whole purpose is to create mini-lives within your whole life.
Each one should strive to be better than the previous.

What shall your next mini-life be?

[M.C.]
January 15, 2014
4:03PM

Letters to Him, 72,

Sometimes I think that I am crazy, like completely mental, because I lack logic yet when I'm in your presence every piece comes together. It sure is a beautiful disaster: Heart vs. Mind.

[M.C.]
January 16, 2014
9:43PM

Margaritë Camaj

Letters to Him, 73,

There is such fascination with the familiar. Investing everything you have into something that you know is stable cannot be conquered. It doesn't mean that you aren't accustomed to change. It just means that you have an obsession with monogamy, not just in relationships, but also in life situations. You are loyal to what you build. I simply have an obsession to change with the familiar-instead of changing with difference frequently. But, they didn't understand me.

[M.C.]
January 17, 2014
8:03PM

Letters to Him, 74,

    Many find it humorous when someone says that they fear nothing. That they fear no outer force. And, if you say that you fear yourself, they look at you strange. Those who doubt don't stop to think that what destroys or heals someone comes from the internal being. It comes from one's own self. One's heart and one's mind is the most fearful. Your mind has the power to deteriorate your soul. Your heart has the ability to blind your vision. In turn, it has the power to damage you physically. However, don't allow that fear to turn you into a robot. Fear is part of humanity. Embrace it.

[M.C.]
January 18, 2014
11:05PM

Letters to Him, 75,

It is in the dark,
>   where I have not only found my aching bones,
> but my hunger for wholeness.
>   So if you shall rob me from that,
run away,
>   For it is all I know.

[M.C.]
January 19, 2014
12:03AM

Letters to Him, 76,

As the rain drops on your skin,
    let it renew you,
Wash away your sins.

As the moon shines on your soul,
    let it renew you,
Allow all your secrets to unfold.

[M.C.]
January 20, 2014
1:03AM

Letters to Him, 77,

Some may say that you've been lost for so long,
    but you're not.
You're on your journey,
    Searching for answers in every corner of, not only the world, but in all the
    corners of your mind.
        You begin to find the beauty in the essence of life.

In your own mind, you learn the definition of you.

[M.C.]
January 21, 2014
2:03AM

Letters to Him, 78,

Just like I'm praying to a God that I'm not sure that I believe in.
    I am trusting my soul when it is only use to grieving.
    And I am loving a love that I don't know if I am needing.

Where would we be without Trust?

[M.C.]
January 22, 2014
3:00AM

Letters to Him, 79,

You committed a lot of sins in this lifetime.

I am well aware.

You spilled out all of your secrets to me at one point or another.

But I am anything from an angel, even though they all think that I am.

Together, though, we destroy hell in order to create our own heaven.

God knows that you and I mean well.

The devil finally meets the angel.

[M.C.]
January 23, 2014
3:00AM

"FUCK!" God is somewhere in my subconscious. He refused to leave me even when I ran away from him. By the way, I am still running.

Letters to Him, 80,

Why do I keep relying on you for happiness, when you keep letting me down, time and time again?
You are like a song that constantly repeats and is forever stuck in my head.
You keep playing the same tune and I keep hoping that the words will be different. You continue to fail me constantly and I am about to eject the CD and finally stop the song from playing. I know I had the power. I guess I just loved how beautifully my mind created you.

[M.C.]
January 24, 2014
4:23AM

Letters to Him, 81,

"I should've listened to my heart. I shouldn't have married him. Now, all I do is toss and turn at night thinking 'what if.' I'm not happy."

I beg of you to not allow this to be you. If there is one thing that you must understand, it is to not marry for anything else but love. Do not marry for money. Do not marry who people think is right for you. Do not marry for comfort. Do not marry because you are getting old. Do not marry for school. Do not marry for religion. Do not marry for security. Do not marry to get away from your problems.

Marriage is fundamental to today's society. And love doesn't die. False entrances into marriages make them fail.

[M.C.]
January 25, 2014
3:00AM

Don't listen to society's views on love. DON'T.

Letters to Him, 82,

You're so blind, you couldn't see her
 love if it looked you straight in your eyes.

You're so deaf, you couldn't hear her
  soul if it whispered to you.

You're so sour, you couldn't taste the
  sweetness of her words if you tried.

You're so cold, you couldn't feel her
  pure skin even with multiple hands.

Her presence is so odorless because
you're use to the smell of evil instead of
  inhaling her imperfect heaven.

Your senses are dead. You aren't
living. You allowed your past to destroy
 you. You are a walking hypocrite.

[M.C.]
January 25, 2014
3:03AM

Letters to Him, 83,

I've developed this obsession with my heart. I have this urge to listen to every little thing that it is trying to tell me. Some might call it illogical, but let me tell you: I am happier than I have ever been. Before, I used to starve my emotions. I never fed them soul food. Now, my emotions are satisfied. They only hunger for more justice of the soul.

[M.C.]
January 26, 2014
3:00AM

Letters to Him, 84,

There is little more that is poetic than a broken man who spills his rough inner core, his soul, in gentle ways, to a broken-hearted, but, good woman.

There is little more that is poetic than a broken woman, who heals his rough soul with a gentle, but mental, glance.

[M.C.]
January 26, 2014
3:03AM

Letters to Him, 85,

You're probably sleeping soundly as I am up, typically, an insomniac. Life isn't fair. It can taste bitter. But hope tastes sweet.

[M.C.]
January 26, 2014
3:13AM

Letters to him, 86,

It was refreshing talking to him. I breathed a bit of fresh air every single time. He didn't have to think. He didn't care about impressing anyone. He just uttered it out. Raw and rare. He spoke not only of pleasure, but also of the artwork of pain. It was straight from the heart. It was always from his heart...

[M.C.]
January 26, 2014
3:23AM

Letters to Him, 87,

I look everywhere and I can't find you. I search in crowds, I search on the streets, and I search within the stars in the night sky. Yet, still, you are nowhere in sight. When I go by the water, close my eyes, and grab my pen and paper:

You come alive in my mind.

[M.C.]
January 26, 2014
3:33AM

Letters to Him, 88,

You're here and I'm there
Far, far away.
Never encountering each other in our bodily presence,
Yet, we quite often meet each other in our minds.

[M.C.]
January 28, 2014
3:00AM

Letters to Him, 89,

She has the happiest smile yet she suffered the most pain.
She has the biggest heart yet it has been drained.

[M.C.]
January 28, 2014
3:03AM

Letters to Him, 90,

There was something about the way that she moved that disrupted his movements.
There was something about the way that she spoke that disrupted his speech.
There was something about the way that she smiled that disrupted his laughter.
There was something about the way that she walked that disrupted his journey.
But, there was something about the way that she left that disrupted his life.

[M.C.]
January 28, 2014
3:13AM

Letters to Him, 91,

They talk about change as if it was this positive thing.

I guess, at times, it can be positive if it arises to give you a better character, but, generally, change terrifies me.

I don't like it.

I fear it.

And, I would probably and most likely bow down to anything, but, change.

My mind wanted to remain the same no matter what.

[M.C.]
January 28, 2014
3:23AM

Letters to Him, 92,

My eyes are burning,
with everything that I see.
I can't tell the difference between love and hate,
and it's blinding me.

[M.C.]
January 29, 2014
3:00AM

Letters to Him, 93,

Crying is beautiful.
Kind of a miracle.
Which is probably why most people fear tears.
It is like something affects your soul so much to the point where your inner emotions leave your body.
The spiritual and the physical connect.
They are beautiful.
I probably can't find a more powerful phenomenon in the human body than tears.

[M.C.]
January 29, 2014
3:03AM

Letters to Him, 94,

Dear God,

I don't ask for much but this I ask of you. Do onto him as he has done to me. Destroy his dreams like he has destroyed mine. Let them take advantage of him like he has done to me. Let him never overcome his obstacles and allow him to suffer in his misery for as long as he lives. God, allow him to demolish himself and drown him in his own convictions. May the person he ends up with cheat, suffocate him with lies, and bury him with her betrayal to a point of no return to mental or physical strength. May he be stripped away from everyone he loves, in the uttermost physical and emotional sense? God, this is what I would ask of you if my heart was like his, but it's not. So I ask for forgiveness on his behalf. Not because he deserves your forgiveness, but because the devil shall never prevail against your forgiving heart.

[M.C.]
January 29, 2014
3:13AM

Letters to Him, 95,

You squint your eyes when you see something meaningful.
You take deep breaths when you're upset.
You laugh from your soul and try to make others happy even when deep inside you're all broken up because the world hurt you.
You're calm though. That is your best quality.

I learned all your facial expressions. I learned all your movements. I know everything about you. I know when you're happy, I know when you're sad, and I know when you're hurt. I know these things because you're me. You are I and I am you. We're one soul in two bodies. So I follow you, without second thought.

The most imperfect phenomenon. One love.

[M.C.]
January 29, 2014
3:23AM

I looked around me and I understood nothing. Space and emptiness was all I saw. My thought processes weren't any of theirs. We were composed of two completely different substances. I wanted to delete the world before I would lose my own soul. I wanted to block everything out and completely immerse myself in the world I create. And, so, I did that.

Letters to Him, 96,

They talk about heaven as if they fear it.
But really, what we should fear is in our presence.
We discriminate, hate, bully, and treat others poorly here.
On earth is really where fear lives.
This is not peace.
War exists both in the struggle of the mental and in the physical.
So when you ask me if I fear heaven, I will look at you strangely and nod my head "no."
I fear earth.
So, I just want to create my own world, alone.
Whoever has strength and character can enter with me.

[M.C.]
January 29, 2014
3:33AM

Letters to Him, 97,

Tonight is extra difficult. There are seconds when I cannot feel you within me.

[M.C.]
January 30, 2014
3:35AM

Letters to Him, 98,

There are moments when I literally feel you escaping my pores.

[M.C.]
January 30, 2014
3:40AM

Letters to Him, 99,

The sun used to talk to me,
so innocent and lovely.
But now the moon whispers,
And seduces me without recovery.

[M.C.]
January 30, 2014
3:43AM

Letters to Him, 100,

I isolated myself from a lot of people, even you at times. I guess you can say something like that.

I liked to be alone a lot, but, at the same time, I didn't feel quite alone when I wrote to you. I don't know. I'm confused.

Somewhere, when I found you, if I even did, I felt a beautiful transformation. That in itself taught me everything.

[M.C.]
January 30, 2014
3:53AM

Letters to Him, 101,

You call me a loner yet, you are the one who always feels alone in a room full of others. At least my thoughts comfort me.

[M.C.]
January 30, 2014
4:03AM

Letters to Him, 102,

Some are so negative about trust.
  How sad.
  They'll never know the power of giving themselves to another fully, with no division in between.
  Inter-tangled.

[M.C.]
January 30, 2014
4:13AM

Letters to Him, 103,

I made a big decision today.
I'm not going to make you the center of my world anymore.
I gave you all of my attention and you turned it into meaningless energy.
I'm sorry, but I'm gone.
Maybe, we will try again at a later date.
Later.

[M.C.]
January 30, 2014
4:23AM

Letters to Him, 104,

I'm lying down confused.
I'm at the same spot that I said I would never be in again, with you.
Do you like taking the life out of me when I give you all of mine?
You're playing games with yourself.
And it is destroying us. But you are me. So, I am talking to myself as well. I guess I destroy myself. My mind plays tricks on me. I told you all. At least I never hid it from you. I was honest.

[M.C.]
January 30, 2014
4:33AM

I'm standing at a place where I am meant to be. I am in New York City. I don't know how or why or when I got here, but all I know is that I am supposed to be here at this exact moment.

I stand here, silently, and my eyes do all of the talking. Both of my pupils directly communicate with my brain as I stare and think about whose soul connects with mine.

I see this man, but he wasn't ordinary. I guess some would call him homeless because his home probably moved around, day by day. Today, I guess, his home is in this dark hole, which is where I stood for the subway daily. Somehow, I felt my soul connect with his and I was at ease. His rugged outfit was parallel to the messed up corners of my mind.

I take a deep breath and decide to look around once again and see who my soul communicates with. I see a young girl, and suddenly I felt déjà vu. I am not sure who she is, but her movements make me feel like I knew her in another life. She is smiling, and she looks at every little thing in this subway, which had all different kinds of evil. Still, she looks at everything with pureness and innocence.

I start to hear the sounds of the next train coming and suddenly, I disconnect with my soul.

February

*These writings still consume me. I find myself intertwined in these lies.
They are lies that you do not even tell. They are the kind of lies that I create
myself because I so deeply want to believe that your heart whispers to mine and
that, in these moments, we are one. Every single time the thought of leaving
your side enters my mind, I completely disperse into something so terribly ugly,
something my soul hates.*

Please stay...

Letters to Him, 105,

But I love him like I love God.
I have a thousand questions, a thousand doubts.
But, he possesses the unknown answers.
I love but fear him, like I do God.
I fear he will leave, but I love him because I trust that he will always come back.

[M.C.]
February 3, 2014
12:03PM

Letters to Him, 106,

"I love you" has become meaningless.
You are not here to give it meaning.
I have forgotten the symbolic presence of those words and I have forgotten
how to allow them to leave my mouth.

[M.C.]
February 5, 2014
8:45 PM

Letters to Him, 107,

He was high, but this time it was a different type of high.
Unlike his past addictions with substances, this substance tasted odd,
just like something that made his mouth water.
He was high off of her soul.
He forgot about his past hurts when he was with her and his worries were silenced.

The ideal movement from past to present.
She was his transition.
He was healed.

[M.C.]
February 7, 2014
12:01PM

Letters to Him, 108,

They say, "His heart is so dirty."

You are all hypocrites.
I see his pure soul.
The rest of you are blind.
He thinks he is selfish, but that is his false misconception.
He loves me more than himself.
It is shown through his actions instead of words.
See, struggles are always placed in destiny.
Timing and obstacles can drown you.
They can make you hate love.
There is no doubt that love brings turbulence, but passion and fate are stronger than any of that.
Some are unlucky and have endured old age in their youth due to "love."
But I refuse to be a part of this society's anti-love movement.
I believe love is greater than what this generation makes it out to be.
Love is a battle, but it conquers all.

[M.C.]
February 9, 2014
10:07PM

Letters to Him, 109,

I have developed this fascination with escape.
It is something I want to do more and more. I'm not sure if it is a good or a bad thing because I can't seem to stay in one place.
I constantly yearn to go away.
I think something might be wrong with me, but this is the first step to admitting something.
I admit it. Ever since you have not been present, I needed help.
I can't do it myself.
The burden is too heavy and I am scarred.

[M.C.]
February 10, 2014
11:09PM

I would rather have my heart bleed to death than to have a valentine with anyone else's breath and fingerprints engraved in my body. My soul could not bare that. I would rather swallow poison than to swallow the taste of his mouth, for it would not be the same as yours. My lips could not speak of that. I would rather burn in fire than to allow his bitter name to leave my lips. My mouth is only familiar with the sound of his name leaving my mouth—not this stranger. My body could not live with that. I would rather know nothing at all than to never know him. Not knowing him is not knowing myself. And, my lungs could breathe with that.

I woke up. I could barely breathe. This was a sign.

I didn't write on Valentine's Day. I just stood in silence to understand my soul more. He was my soul.

Forgive me if you are all a little confused about my view on love. I don't think that anyone has every loved me back in the same way that I have loved them. But, then again, I cannot blame them. My love is extremely strong, so strong, that it can often kill people's souls—causing them to leave.

Now, I write to you about one of the few forms of love that I have ever known. The love of a father and daughter. All love stems from there.

Letters to Him, 110,

I watched him carefully even though growing up I was confused. Everyone loved words. They loved to tell each other how they left. They loved expressing their emotions. But he was different from the average man. He didn't tell me what to do. He didn't tell me how to act. You know, like, he didn't tell me what to do with my life. He didn't brag about what he had. He was humble. He lived in a small apartment in the Bronx even though he deserved way more just to give me a better life. He stood quiet. I won't lie, there were times were I hated it and it saddened me. But today, I hold that dear. Instead, my father showed me beauty. And by that, I mean that he taught me how to live without forcing me to act a certain way. He taught me the importance of a man to show you that they love you instead of just telling you.

[M.C.]
February 15, 2014
12:03PM

I am understanding my mind and heart, slowly...

Letters to Him, 111,

If I can give you one piece of advice, it would be to not frown. People go their separate ways all the time, even if it is just two complete strangers holding the door for one another or walking by each other on the street. Even if it is just a simple glance you exchange with someone you know nothing about. What is beautiful is that in that exact moment, the other individual was supposed to be there. Do you get it? It comes from necessity.

In that exact second, the other person was supposed to cross your path. Maybe that is why you didn't do that thing you had to do earlier. Or maybe that is why you didn't wake up to your alarm clock. Even though you are now strangers, they entered your life for a purpose. God brought them to you in order to help each other figure out something about yourself, whether it is good or bad. You all gave me life. I love them all for that.

[M.C.]
February 16, 2014
10:11PM

Letters to Him, 112,

The raw and pure beauty in her was that she had hope,
when they had none.

[M.C.]
February 16, 2014
11:01PM

But, if I love God so much, why do I stay questioning Him about my path? "Stop it, Merzi. Keep ignoring Him." And ignore Him, I did. But, was I really ignoring Him? He gave me the strength to write about you even when I was at my weakest. I always compared him to God. Maybe he has not arrived yet because I did not allow God to arrive yet. Perhaps. "Shut up, Merzi." There goes my mind again.

Letters to Him, 113,

Oh what a beautiful tragedy death is,
With every breath, a piece of you deteriorates and you are closer to the end.
You die many times within your actual life span.
But the fairness in this is that rebirth follows after every exhalation...

[M.C.]
February 17, 2014
12:03AM

Letters to Him, 114,

I want him to go to my past.

I want to go to his past as well.

Walking together through it, holding hands.

Not because of trust issues, not because of insecurity, not because of instigation: nothing related to negativity.

But, so that, together, we can go to the depths up hell, destruction, heartache, what made you laugh, what made you cry, how you grew up, what your struggles and fears were. We can know each other thoroughly.

Only then, will we be able to have that bond, that unconditional love, that will get us through the future.

[M.C.]
February 17, 2014
4:07AM

Letters to Him, 115,

I know he loves me.
But you guys can't blame me for questioning.
It is hard to want that because I don't know love.
Love, to people like me, was always misconstrued.
Love, to people like me, was ways misunderstood and misinterpreted.
God confuses me, just like you do.

[M.C.]
February 18, 2014
12:03PM

Letters to Him, 116,

Passionate people are rare, but they are to be admired because they are filled with consistency.

I either love something whole-heartedly and let nothing come between us, or my body shivers with the distasteful hate that you have forced me to develop for you.

[M.C.]
February 18, 2014
1:01PM

One day I love you. One day I cannot even find love at all. Desperation.

Letters to Him, 117,

If I trust God so much, why do I keep doubting my path?
If I love them so much, why do I keep questioning their presence?
And if I miss you in my life, why can't
I feel your existence in the physical?

[M.C.]
February 19, 2014
2:03AM

Letters to Him, 118,

Pain demands to be felt.
So I always loved to feel it.
It gave me energy. It gave me fuel.
But this pain was different.
This time it was unbearable.
I felt weird tingles throughout my body and all of my movements were halted.
Everything was immobile.
I felt as if every bone in my body was breaking. I became completely paralytic.

[M.C.]
February 19, 2014
3:00AM

The days of this month have gone by terribly slow. There were many times where I have almost lost myself. There were times where I was not sure if my soul could endure any more pain. I tried to stay away from writing because I thought that I could escape you. I tried to make friends with everything other than the pen and the paper, but every single time I did that, I just became more and more lost. I had to face it. There was no way that you could escape me.

March

Keep reading. It gets pretty deep this month. Remember, sometimes, you don't lose people. Sometimes, they remain within your soul forever.

And I used to have this irrational fear of people leaving, until I realized that they were just souls who came into your life to make you realize something. If it weren't for these souls, who bring secret messages from an outside force, whatever that force is, there would probably be no way that you would've figured it out yourself. I think that we are very powerful alone, as individuals, but the power of the universe brings us what we need at the exact time we need it. The souls who stay have not finished their mission and those who left, have. I call this calculated timing.

Letters to Him, 119,

I tried telling them, but they wouldn't be able to understand unless they could somehow enter my spirituality. It was pointless to utter words that weren't enough. How could I have written words to possibly express her essence, her character, and what she stood for? She stood for something that was perfectly immaculate. The world gave her reasons to give up.

At times, I was probably at fault for contributing to that, especially with how heavily I am involved in my own world. However, she didn't let that make her give up. She looked at it right in the face and kept moving. She said it couldn't break her. You know what? There were times where I have wanted to give up. She showed me how giving up was not an option.

When I was emotionally weak, she showed me what it was like to be emotionally strong. She had plenty to brag about and not once did anything but humility leave her mouth. Her touch was gentle, but she knew the appropriate times to make it strong. My mother is a woman who cannot be conquered. And I will forever thank her for passing that gift onto me.

[M.C.]
March 1, 2014
11:03PM

Letters to Him, 120,

Maybe he is the reason I never give up.
Maybe he is the reason I have all this emotional strength.
Maybe he is the reason I often question the world.
Maybe he is the reason I have an old soul.
Maybe he is the reason I'm empathetic to others.
Maybe he is the reason I love with all my soul.
Maybe he is the reason 3 is my favorite number.
Maybe he is the reason I have an obsession with the 80's.
Maybe he is the reason why I follow the way back to God even after I doubt Him.
Tribute to my brother, Martin. I keep him locked in my soul, like I do you.

[M.C.]
March 3, 2014
7:05PM

Letters to Him, 121,

  She started to look at the world differently.

Her eyes became brighter and her vision became clearer.

She had a look of awe as she walked around, curious as to what she would discover next, what would make her happy.

Limitless and unstoppable: her mind was strong, but her soul was gentle.

Her pure heart and pure intentions spilled out of her mouth, from every breath she inhaled and exhaled.

We'll never be fully innocent since we are not children anymore, but we are learning to reverse the dirt that was thrown at us by those stealing our innocence. They chose to remain in the world with dirty hands.

We fight against this. We live. We are free.

We are finding bursts of innocence in a world constantly trying to lock us in chains.

[M.C.]
March 4, 2014
9:07PM

Letters to Him, 122,

Why their souls didn't align:
There was little more beautiful than her silence.
There was little more ugly than his words.

[M.C.]
March 4, 2014
11:03PM

It was a Saturday night and there she sat, at home with her face buried in her books next to her cat and her favorite pair of pajamas that she never wanted to throw out due to the memories and comfort that they gave her. I kept writing. I thought of love, as I always did. And I didn't just think of love, I thought of you. It was beautiful how you made an appearance to my soul over and over again no matter what. You allowed me to not give up. I am starting to believe that you will appear even though you haven't arrived yet. My mind and heart still fought. I don't think that they will ever stop fighting.

Letters to Him, 123,

We're all hypocrites.

We want love, but we destroy it when we have it.

We want faith, but we constantly question.

We want trust, but we say we trust no one.

We want good company, but we crave isolation.

We want health, but we harm our bodies.

We want the spiritual goods, but we desire materials.

We want soul food, but we feast off of negative desires.

We want light, but we search for darkness.

We want, but we don't give in return.

We are humans, but we have forgotten our humanity.

We're all hypocrites.

[M.C.]
March 5, 2014
3:03AM

Letters to Him, 124,

Timing.
They say that time is our enemy:
It wastes too quickly,
It depletes suddenly,
and it is always off.
You would think that we can never grasp time, so we end up blaming it.
Perhaps, our mentality is off.
Perhaps, we have enough time.
Perhaps, time is our ally.
Perhaps, we fault in always questioning time.
Perhaps, timing turns out to be perfect in the end.
Perhaps.

[M.C.]
March 5, 2014
5:03AM

What a sad thought it is to think that nothing is certain, to think that nothing is stable, to think that everything is temporary. I cannot drown my heart in these thoughts.

Letters to Him, 125,

Something terrible is killing me inside.

That is why I need books to put me in another life.

That is why I need to escape somewhere other than the comfortable.

That is why I need to drive for miles until I know nothing around me except for the same exact emptiness that I feel. At least, there, I feel like I have something in common with my surroundings.

That is why I need to turn the music up so loud until my thoughts drown so deep that I can't think.

I've perfected the silencing of the loudness in my mind.

[M.C.]
March 6, 2014
1:03AM

She was always trying to save everyone else, and never stopped to think that maybe, just maybe, she should try and save herself.
I did, through my writings.

Letters to Him, 126,

It was instinctive.

Memorization.

We just knew.

It is like we knew what the other was going to do before the other even moved.

It is like we knew what the other was going to say without even speaking a word.

It is like we knew when the other was crying without even shedding a tear.

It is like we knew when the other would laugh without even making eye contact.

Isn't it beautiful when you can just recognize yourself in another human's body?

It is like we just knew.

[M.C.]
March 6, 2014
2:01AM

Letters to Him, 127,

He told me that he would meet me in a conflicting time, in a conflicting world.
He said he would always return at a time of confusion.
There was a while where I thought that he lied, where he didn't tell the truth.
But my conceptions were heavily flawed.
He returned for a very short time each day.
You always returned to my soul.
I remember.

[M.C.]
March 6, 2014
9:03AM

Letters to Him, 128,

They think that I haven't found you yet, but I have.
  Although you may not be here physically, I am certain that I have found
  you spiritually.
  I have almost learned who I am, and through that, I have found you.
  Through hundreds of laughs and hundreds of tears, we have come to
  understand each other.
  You have been through all of my struggles with me.
Possibly, you have been through similar battles: different battle variations of
love and of the self.
  I've known you for thousands of years.
  I've known you for many different lifetimes.
  I've loved you in a previous life.
  I'm just waiting for you to appear in this one.

[M.C.]
March 9, 2014
1:03AM

Letters to Him, 129,

The raindrops fell on us.
My mind memorized your thoughts.
My body learned your language.
My soul understood you.
At that moment, we weren't human anymore.
We gave that up.
We were solely remains that promised to be faithful in mind, body, and soul.
One was enough.

[M.C.]
March 9, 2014
1:15AM

Letters to Him, 130,

He wasn't exactly God's favorite,
but he has enough to be considered his strongest soldier.
He didn't speak in big, fancy words,
but he has enough to speak my soul's language.
He wasn't filled with riches to cover me in jewels,
but he has enough in his inner being to make me feel like royalty.
He wasn't covered in designer clothes,
but he has enough hardships stored in his mind to label him a classic.
His heart wasn't whole,
but we have enough broken pieces to fit in each other's puzzle.
He was always enough.

[M.C.]
March 9, 2014
1:17AM

Letters to Him, 131,

When we find a deep love, we tend to forget that we are humans.
We doze off. We fall into a non-reality.
Our souls are spiritual and because of that, we think that we can't break.
We think we are strong enough.
We believe in illusionary visions.
But our souls, as invincible as they are, are kept within our bodies. How ironic.
How can something so invincible think that it can last inside a human?
We are so tangible. So weak.
Something so fragile as our bones, that can break;
our skin, that can bruise;
our veins, that can bleed.
How are we expected to hold something that cannot be touched?
And when we finally do wake up from that non-reality:
This is the tragedy of the human being.

[M.C.]
March 9, 2014
1:23AM

Letters to Him, 132,

I could say that I am falling in love with the spring:
The way that the birds fly free, knowing their destination,
The way the flowers bloom so colorfully,
The way the birds sing a song,
The way the sun shines happily,
But, I would be a liar.
I fell in love with something else, and I can't escape it.
I fell in love with the way I found the essence of myself in the midst of the dark, cold, and bitter nights.
Somewhere in these moments, I conditioned myself to warmth.
I fell in love with the naked tree branches that are forever engraved in my memory as if they were cracks in a cement wall.
It was within these sights that I found hope and I stripped myself of color so I could understand what was black.
Eventually, we have to face the fact that we are human.

[M.C.]
March 10, 2014
1:01AM

Letters to Him, 133,

It has been a while.

    The more I tried to convince him that I loved darkness,

    The more reason he gave me to crave the light.

    The more I tried to convince him that I was bruised,

    The more reason he gave me to heal my mind, body, and soul.

    The more I tried to convince him that I'm cold,

The more reason he gave me to show him warmth.

And the more I tried to convince him that I know nothing but hate,

    The more reason he gave me to love.

        My heart tore open.

[M.C.]
March 10, 2014
1:13AM

Letters to Him, 134,

Preferably, meet me on a gray cloudy day, somewhere in between the rain.
Meet me somewhere you don't typically go when you're happy.
Meet me on your worst day, where you go to hide away from all your problems.
Meet me at a time when your heart no longer beats.
For then, if we shall meet, we meet at a foundation that is crumbled,
And if we are meant to be, we could help each other fix the cracks so we can return to the same place and understand the sun.

[M.C.]
March 10, 2014
1:17AM

Margaritë Camaj

Letters to Him, 135,

He didn't know the meaning of life until he crossed paths with her.
He didn't know the depth of innocence until he knew her.
He didn't know the essence of kindness until he looked in her eyes.
He didn't know the nature of honesty until they conversed.
He didn't know the significance of faithfulness until she never left his side.
He didn't know the importance of love until her heart stopped beating.
But he didn't know the tragedy of death until he lost her.

[M.C.]
March 10, 2014
1:33AM

**I had another nightmare last night. He wrote
a letter to me through my soul...**

*She stopped my entire pathway of air: the part where my lungs were
supposed to breathe in and out. I didn't get it and I will never understand
the narcotics of the atoms that created her. They put a warning label on
a pack of cigarettes labeling death, but they never put a warning label
on her. Why didn't they? I've been smoking for years and nothing has
happened, but in a matter of seconds she was able to stop my whole
world: stop my movements, stop my breathing, and stop my heart.*

Letters to Him, 136,

It is this.

It is this moment. It is this present. It is this breath.

It is the way I allow my heart to beat freely.

It is the way my skin fears no danger.

It is the way every breath consumes fresh air.

It is that fuel of happiness that allows you to conquer anything.

There is no fear of crashing.

I am walking as if I were running.

I am laughing as if I will never know a tear.

Not in the next second. Not tomorrow.

No limitations. Now.

This. My heart beats for this.

[M.C.]
March 11, 2014
6:13AM

I fear it will end. "Stop it Merzi." There goes my mind again.

Letters to Him, 137,

God is my artist. He drew me with a black pen and allowed me to paint myself precisely between the lines. I love Him.

[M.C.]
March 12, 2014
2:03AM

"*Whoa. Merzi*," My mind is very loud again. Did you just tell God I love you? I snapped out of it and tried to listen to my heart. The closer I was getting to him, the closer I was getting to God....

Letters to Him, 138,

He said that he noticed the way that I love more when I hurt. In a way, it is true. I feel it more. I embrace it more. I am broken, but, it is the only thing I hold close even though it is so unknown and unfamiliar to me. It is the only thing that can heal me. Maybe I want to feel hurt. Maybe that is the only way I can come close to the exposure of love. Love is my cure. It heals me.

[M.C.]
March 13, 2014
3:01AM

Letters to Him, 139,

I was down and I didn't really know where else to turn, but he slowly picked me up. By down, I don't mean slightly fallen. I mean completely on the floor, lying there hopelessly when no one else understood the depths of my soul. But, he understood it in some weird way.

It was weird because he wasn't trying to tweak it or change it, which was what I was used to. He was just trying to expose it. It was just like the sun was trying to expose the bottom of the ocean, finding the seashells and all of that stuff. He didn't step on my soul just like the sand underneath the ocean water, where your foot leaves an imprint and crushes one's soul.

Instead, he gravitated in between the air and the water. He just floated there. My love for him resides somewhere there.

It is hidden, just like the line between the water and the air. You know it exists. You just can't visibly see it.

[M.C.]
March 13, 2014
4:05AM

My heart was like an empty piece of paper. It was waiting for your mind to connect with mine and have all your words leave permanent ink marks on it. But, you left a terrible mess. You left permanent ink all over, the non-erasable kind. Then, you picked up and left.

How do you expect me to clean this up?

My heart will no longer return to the empty piece of paper you found before your arrival. They are all written up, torn, and scary looking.

I fear, as I shake, that my heart shall never forgive you and that you shall always remain there, silently, but, hatefully, because I will never return to who I was. I think you changed me for the worse and I am too full.

I woke up, shaking. I ran around my room until I found the pen and the paper. That was just a nightmare. I tried to write more poetry down and allow you to spill onto the paper just to make sure that I didn't lose you. I had to make sure that I didn't lose my ability to write. This dream was too real.

Letters to Him, 140,

Is what the subconscious touches real?
But when does heaven begin?
And is hell just a concept we create?

These illusions are just signs brought to us by something greater, whatever it is that we believe in. Something exists to connect all the dots together: to perfectly align them. It is possible that when we close our eyes, we fall into a floating state. Here, our minds go to work and our hearts softly beat. Our dreams connect so that sleep can give our hearts the necessity of inner peace for a short while. Maybe we escape somewhere unknown for a few hours: somewhere calm, somewhere beautiful, and somewhere heavenly. Maybe it is throughout the subconscious that our minds and hearts balance each other out, in a way.

[M.C.]
March 15, 2014
9:03AM

I went by the water quite a lot during this month.
I needed fulfillment. I needed you.

Letters to Him, 141,

This. I am still when I am here. I feel one with the elements on the earth: air, water, dirt, and fire. The way the air gently blows my bones into place. The way the water synchronizes my thoughts. The way the dirt reminds me that the most ugly and the dirtiest things can be the most beautiful. The way the fire burns all my miseries and all my worries so that I shall forget they existed. Nature allows me to flourish. It calls me, by my name, symbolically and silently. I never doubt it. My physical and spiritual beings are in sync. My thoughts align and everything seems to make sense. Calmness and solitude. This.

[M.C.]
March 16, 2014
10:01PM

Letters to Him, 142,

She was as cold as ice.

After meeting her, many ran, especially the weak and intimidated.

He was different.

Non-hesitantly, he speeded towards her with a burning inferno that melted her whole being until it broke all of her walls down.

That was all it took: a man with a burning mind longing for emotions.

[M.C.]
March 19, 2014
11:03PM

I felt my skin. I was still cold. I still couldn't tell if I was awake or asleep when I wrote all of this. I feel as if my mind is taking me to places where my heart doesn't recognize, so it sleeps throughout the whole thing.

Letters to Him, 143,

They sang to each other through mystery.
They searched for the unknown through the tangible.
They knew each other better than they had thought.

[M.C.]
March 20, 2014
1:07AM

Letters to Him, 144,

This was different. It wasn't my skin that got goose bumps or chills. This time, it was my mind.

[M.C.]
March 20, 2014
2:03AM

Letters to Him, 145,

He knew that the green tea at Starbucks was my favorite: unsweetened & bitter. He knew my favorite color: black. He knew what I needed when "You Found Me" by The Fray played. He knew it meant silence, analyzing, & disappearance into my own world. He knew my calm when my world was a bit shaken: writing.

I didn't find any of this to be a big deal though. Everyone knew this, right? It was ordinary, right? I think that was the tragedy of it all. I never paid attention. I was the type of person that easily became lost in my own world and I, sometimes, became trapped there. My world made me blind to yours. So that, when he revealed the reason for my love for the bitter; my love for black: beauty in simplicity; how I daily starved to hear "You Found Me" because it gave me hope; and how he was deeply saddened when I was lost in words because he realized that I couldn't reciprocate in speech. My pieces went missing. I wasn't connected.

[M.C.]
March 20, 2014
3:01AM

It is about to get really deep. Stay tuned. My soul
felt his presence a little extra tonight.

Letters to Him, 146,

I remember the first time we spoke. Your words spoke to my brain so loud that my previous memory of anyone and anything else was quickly and completely wiped: eliminated. But, I think, the most important was when my heart realized that every word you uttered was like blood leaving your mouth so that you can fill the parts of me that didn't function anymore.

You were so raw and so full of truth. I was stuck and frozen in time for a while. But, it didn't leave me abandoned for a long time.

You wanted to unfreeze me and you did. But, I am frozen again. However, do not panic. This time it is a good kind of frozen. You are frozen inside of me. I could not forget you even if I tried.

You held my time.

What perfect timing.

[M.C.]
March 23, 2014
3:05AM

Letters to Him, 147,

    The moon never leaves. It is always hidden and unnoticeable. Only those who remember to remember it, do. Just like you, I wonder if it tries to speak to me and tells me not to forget it while the sun is shining. He tells me to wait, patiently, and he will re-appear every night. I guess this was a trust thing, and I was not sure if I was quite ready to make that kind of commitment yet.

[M.C.]
March 23, 2014
4:05AM

Letters to Him, 148,

If you caught all my teardrops, you could have converted them into gold that ran through your blood stream.

Instead, you let them fall into a navigable river, where they have flowed into the hands of others and now I am lost in a body of water, so consuming, that you will never find me again.

[M.C.]
March 23, 2014
4:09AM

Letters to Him, 149,

When they ask me if I have a tattoo, I will never say "no" again. Your fingerprints are all over my heart. Your voice runs through my veins. It is so chilling that it is permanent. Your legacy will be inherited through my soul even when nature no longer allows my heart to beat. So, what is a tattoo with ink that deteriorates when your body decomposes? Next time they ask, I will say yes. I would be a deceiver, a liar, and a hypocrite to ever deny that. You are my tattoo.

[M.C.]
March 23, 2014
5:01AM

Letters to Him, 150,

You never stopped being my moon. The moon never leaves even when it is hidden and unnoticeable. You just didn't appear in the daytime. It was invisible, but, when you appeared, it was always so full and lovely. I noticed you, even when you thought that I would forget you. The sun played with my mind and tried to persuade me into forgetting about you. The sun would shine brighter than ever so that it could blind my eyes to what my heart felt. When you weren't here, my heart, my mind, and my soul became paralyzed. I could not move. I could not grow. You were my movement. We go against every rule placed in front of you and I, yet they still could not stop us from growing.

I told you not to doubt the strength of my mind. I am not weak. I never forgot to remember you.

If I had denied this, the universe would have died. It would have never aligned perfectly. Nothing would have made sense.

[M.C.]
March 24, 2014
10:01PM

Letters to Him, 151,

Perhaps it was the way that your eyes always found mine when my vision became lost. Perhaps it was the way your words prevented my mind from losing itself.

Perhaps it was the way that your body became my home when my head was placed against your heartbeat. Perhaps it was the way your touch was filled with such passion that it quickly burned the most frozen and cold parts of my soul.

In these little moments, something undying occurred. You have silenced, calmed, and healed me. This was something like a fire that is constantly being attempted to be put out, but never has it succeeded.

You found me. Now, the hard part: stay.

[M.C.]
March 24, 2014
10:09PM

"Merzi, he didn't find you. But he will find you. Stop it, mind."

Letters to Him, 152,

I am not quite sure what was worse: being in a place so loud and feeling complete silence and isolation within or living in silence when your insides want to scream out loud.

[M.C.]
March 25, 2014
11:01PM

Margaritë Camaj

She spoke through her mind and that transferred into her eyes. She
sat there and started telling him her story as he tried to read her
emotions that were yelling through silence. He did not have a clue
how to react. He didn't know of all the seconds, minutes, hours, days,
months, and years that had drained her. He took her hand and placed
his two fingers on her wrist. He was finally getting some vital signs.
She was dead and he was breathing life into her. She went through
it all alone, but how beautiful was it that she no longer had to.
"FUCK!" I can't take these nightmares anymore. They were
getting the best of me. I think I was getting closer to him.

Letters to Him, 153,

What a blessing it is to have someone understand the language your eyes speak without having to utter a word. That person becomes your vision. Perhaps that is why we become blinded when we love. Our lover becomes our thief, stealing all perception.

[M.C.]
March 26, 2014
7:03AM

These past months have been nothing but pain for me. I'm sorry if I have been all over the place, but in reality, this is how my mind works. It jumps from one thing to another, but my contradiction comes into play again. No matter how much my mind has scrambled its thoughts, it has managed to stay stable. My mind has managed to stay the same and not change for anyone or anything. It has remained the same for him. They could steal everything away from me, but they couldn't steal him away from my soul.

And maybe you have stolen all of my perception.

My soul knows more than I ever will.

He is my soul.

And maybe, just maybe, now, God exists. It is possible...

April

My interaction with everyone has become hostile. Physically, my body
functions. Everyone sees me, but they don't see what I have become. Maybe
they do, and I refuse to accept and notice my own self. I have deteriorated to
the core of my bones. My existence has almost become inferior to his. I don't
know where or how this happened, but I find my mind trying to convince
myself of everything except for the fact that I am alone. My mind is so strong,
but my heart: it is terribly weak. Somehow, they balance each other out.
I try to believe in my words, but my words have dragged me to
this position. I have become engulfed in them. I have become a
theory. I have isolated reality. I have closed off the world. This is
how people form habits. This is how I formed this habit.

I am almost ashamed at what you are about to read and come to
understand. I almost gave up my soul. I almost settled. I almost
went against what was written. I left God. I left my fate. I disowned
my destiny. I had almost forgotten about you. Believe me, when I
say that I have searched a whole lot. I have searched people, places,
and things. But, the people were the most difficult to overcome.
So I sat with them, I had conversations, but, was I really talking to them? Was
I really living at all? I gave them no piece of me even when they gave me all of
theirs. I'm ashamed, but I had to do what I had to do. I promise, I have never
betrayed your love. How could I? When everything that I did was somehow
in your name. It was as if I had the ability to place a mask around my heart
disallowing any entrance from the outside world. You were trapped inside.
And, I don't understand it. That is why I hate it most. It was as if time froze.
Time meant nothing. It is quite a tragedy how I have allowed my days to

pass without alteration. And I remember, quite vividly, the hour and time
that I placed my mind in metal bars: allowing no escape. I even saw him in
God: invisible yet I am the product of Him. At the same time I wanted to
forget Him, I forgot God. I didn't know that God was showing me the path of
return to Him, while revealing the same man. It is you. It was you all along.
I have met little pieces of the same man in different people. So, I
cut their souls apart until I could get that piece that resembled you
back. I didn't want them to have any part that resembled him.
I'm sorry. Don't hate me. I have danced with time so beautifully that I
have given myself completely to something that cannot be touched.
Now, don't tell me that this short amount of time defines the
soul. Don't tell me this time meant nothing compared to history.
For no amount of history stands a chance with this force.
I, I have met your soul in different time periods. We are the
same. We are stronger. I am convinced. For, it could have been
one second, and that second would kill the weakest love.
I...I...I love you.

Letters to Him, 154,

The chills that moved through my body, when he declared his love to me, were so strong that roots started to grow inside of me. And every time he departed, he thought that the roots would stop growing, but they didn't. They needed water and he didn't provide that. Maybe that is why she constantly searched for the ocean. Her soul craved for him and she believed that he was hidden somewhere in depths of the waters.

[M.C.]
April 5, 2014
1:03AM

Ideally, I just want to sit and talk until the sun comes up with an iced green tea in my right hand and my left hand tangled in yours. I want to lay here until a comfortable silence appears in the distance and we keep getting closer and closer until we fully grasp it. I want to lay here until every wall has been broken down and we can rebuild ourselves again. I want to lay here until my touch learns every part of your spiritual being. I want to know you like you know yourself: flaws included. I want to lay with you until you help me understand myself because, without you, I am missing a part of who I am. I am not whole. I am only a piece. I want to lay here with you until you know what my simplicity includes of. I do not care to know about fancy things when it comes to love. Please come in your most raw and simple form. Please come with flaws, fears, and ugliness. Do not come embellished in lies. And, I want to stay there, perfectly still, until your soul bleeds into mine and we create our own world. *Let's escape, let's escape...*

Letters to Him, 155,

They told me to not place my peace in a human, but they did not know the power that his love had on me. You are the only drug that I would ever try until my bones deteriorate: until my blood runs dry. I would pick chaos over your abandonment any day.

[M.C.]
April 6, 2014
10:01PM

Letters to Him, 156,

I drown you in me. My purpose in life is to love you for I know no other the way that I know you. Without you, I am not free.

[M.C.]
April 9, 2014
11:03PM

The thought of escaping from you leaves me with chills, ones that almost make me gasp for air as I see the moon disappear. I am too certain that the sunlight will come, a new day had begun, and you have fallen from my nightmare.

I woke up. You weren't in my nightmares at all. You never were. Were you even in my reality? "Stop it Merzi. There goes your mind again."

Letters to Him, 157,

    If your heart ever feels a little too empty, know I will deplete mine to give you a pulse. I will not judge you. I want to know you at your lowest. I have been very low and I understand the pain. Purity is a form of perception and while they might not believe you are pure, I firmly hold on to my perception.

    To me, your heart is not dirty, but it is, instead, beautifully clean. It holds my soul and it is impossible that it should be unworthy. You should know that my cells have been crushed into tiny bits and pieces before you. And, you should know that the smallest atoms that compose me have been disordered. My chemicals have decomposed before. I get it. I understand your pain.

    Let us try to rearrange them to the best of our ability. Together.

[M.C.]
April 10, 2014
7:05AM

    Margaritë Camaj

Letters to Him, 158,

Keep an eye out for people who are able to remain constant and stable through changes. They have a strong character. The wind may blow in many different directions, and although, they love variations and differentiations, they remain grounded. They see the stars, but their feet are on the ground. They are faithful to where they came from and to those around them. The weak should fear them and the strong see them. Nothing can conquer them. Nothing. Not even broken love.

[M.C.]
April 21, 2014
1:07AM

I felt like I was getting closer with each day that
passed by. I was fighting harder than ever.

Letters to Him, 159,

He knew my most simple moves and the way that I breathed too well. Going against him or straying in the opposite direction would be a form of internal suicide: the kind where your heart doesn't stop beating, but the song becomes unfamiliar and devastatingly ugly. Not knowing him would mean that the bodily organs work, but the chest feels too heavy, as if something is missing. Being alive becomes a paradox. That was the scariest thing in placing my fate in his hands. I was independent in all other things except for this. I became so trusting that it became terrifying. Trust was a stranger to me before this. Before you. He knew me before I even fully knew myself. That was rare.

[M.C.]
April 23, 2014
2:03AM

Letters to Him, 160,

I always felt as if people were grabbing parts and pieces of me and pulling me in hundreds of different directions. They didn't trust my movements and didn't see how dense and overwhelmed I was. You were different. You just let me be still and loved me that way. If I couldn't see the beauty in that, I would be lacking something heavy. I would be lacking something in my soul. Thank God, I wasn't.

[M.C.]
April 27, 2014
3:01AM

I felt extra guilty today. I felt like I used God, in a way. Why was it that when I felt like I was going away from him and that he never existed that God felt so far away? I couldn't even think of God at times. I didn't even want to have anything to do with Him. Why is it that when I feel like I am getting closer to you that I am getting closer to God? I don't know if this was God's way of telling me something or if this was just my mind playing tricks on me. Whatever it was, it felt strange.

These thoughts were going through my head as I was watching these planes fly in and out. They kind of remind me of my emotions and the ability to enforce and control them: just like a start and go button. Sometimes they shout go but they quickly come to a complete halt. I ask myself why this is the case, but many times, I am hesitant to explain it.

Then, I think of my childhood and my tragic experiences that I had gone through. Other times, I think of my adolescence and the difficulty in which I had endured. But, then I think of love and what I had done to try to hold on to it. I was just so scared that it was not within my touch. I still lived with the fear that there was not much that I can do to keep it. That is when I kept digging and digging inside of my body. Quickly, I tried to free any uncontrolled thought or any uncontrolled feeling so that I can finally have full control over the emotions that I had once misunderstood.

I realized that I can fully come to a mutual understanding with them once I realized that my emotions were in possession of their owner, me. Maybe my heart was starting to understand my mind. Maybe, they would learn to get along after all.

Letters to Him, 161,

I have one thing on my mind that has been weighing me down. I fear that there will come a time when I am not able to write. I fear that there will come a time when the power of you within me stops working. I might have run out of things to say...or things to write, to you.

[M.C.]
April 28, 2014
5:05PM

I struggle to write this down, but I want to share it with you. I almost hate myself for this, but I almost got tired of your soul tonight. I hate myself for it, but tonight, I almost said goodbye to you.

I almost wrote one last thing: maybe we'll meet in another life. Thankfully, I took control of my emotions and I stopped myself. **I was quite weak tonight.**

Letters to Him, 162,

He looked at her as if she were a rose.

The beauty lied in how he embraced every single one of her thorns. One, by one, he dissected every scar that touched her mind. He came closer than anyone ever has.

He came without hesitation, without doubt.

He came with a healing power. He came with a force so strong that only a certain type of God could possess. A God she never met before.

He smelled their scent, saw the beauty in their imperfections, heard the pain, swallowed the bitterness, and felt their sting in the most horrific way.

One day, he dropped the rose on the floor.

You see, he is imperfect too, human: incapable of being immaculate, full of insecurities, and chaos.

The rose slowly died. She only came back to life when it rained, resuscitating herself. He taught her a beautiful gift: how to water her own thorns. She learned to love herself.

[M.C.]
April 29, 2014
3:03AM

I'm sorry I didn't write as much this month. I felt like I needed to feel more. I needed to know what it felt like to live without the pen just for a little bit. I felt like I spent so much time hiding my face in a pen and paper in the months before that I tried to live life a little more. No matter how much I tried, I still found myself drowned in you. I couldn't get away. You have spent so much time in my soul. So much, that the more I loved myself, the more I learned to love you.

Ps. The month of May might be a little slow as well. I am trying to absorb everything. I am trying to figure out how to live again and where I will end up. I am constantly trying to figure everything out—EVERYTHING.

May

I don't know. I just don't. Okay? The days were coming sooner than I had expected. The time was coming closer and I still wasn't sure about what I was feeling. I don't know what is going on, but I do know that all of my feelings are making me feel uneasy. It feels as if I am feeling everything at the same time: all at once. How was it possible that I spent seconds, minutes, hours, days, and months waiting for this time to return and now the emotion of fear is at its strongest point? How is it that I can allow one emotion to have so much power over me and to control me in such a way that I become confused about whether I want to return? Fear takes over me so much, at times, that I almost become immune to you. Fear almost causes me to block you out. Almost. But it never does.

Letters to Him, 163,

    I am sorry for wanting to take your soul. I place my hand on my heart I and swear that I didn't want to change it. I didn't want to change my heart because then that would mean that I would have to change yours. But, you have to believe me. You have to believe that it was never my intention to change what I was feeling. I swear. My intentions were never unclean. My intentions were never to hurt you or do you harm, but I realized that I might have been doing that because I didn't take care of myself that well. I drained myself. At times, I drained my own soul, and I had such trouble understanding it. But, maybe I just wanted to find more of myself because there wasn't truth in what I had already known about myself. I always saw more potential and I didn't want to give up. I guess I was never satisfied. Maybe, I had confused your soul with mine. There will come a time where we might meet again at the perfect timing, whether it is like a heaven or hell.

[M.C.]
May 3, 2014
3:00AM

It is about 9:07 PM. I never really looked at the clock until after I finished writing, but now I did. Everything is starting to feel a bit more calculated. Maybe it is the anxiety that I have because I know what might or might not come out of the end of these letters. I don't know what will happen when I return, but I do know that it is slowly taking over my humanity and I am starting to feel like I am a ghost. I look at the clock and I feel it again. It feels like I have lost everything. I have nothing spiritual left. Random feelings and random nights. I guess I'm still living in fear and I have yet to overcome it.

Letters to Him, 164,

    I almost threw out all my pieces until he taught me to realize that my pieces were worth more than me being whole. He made love to me without getting physical. He had the ability to talk to my mind and get me naked without me taking one piece of clothing off. We were two naked souls in each other's presence and we never knew, before this, that we were intertwined in the other. We had one purpose in life: we had lived for the other. He was omnipotent and powerful.

[M.C.]
May 5, 2014
3:03AM

Letters to Him, 165,

Let the night put you to sleep so silently that you can hear your own heart beating and so that I can hear my lungs breathe for you.

[M.C.]
May 7, 2014
12:03PM

Where you are is where my soul is and where my soul is flourishes endlessly, for you. And I think that you were concrete, like where I first learned what love was in the midst of chaos. I fell in love with the harshest, yet most beautiful part of the city. It was so ugly that it became a work of art in my eyes. I always looked at things in a different light. What they saw was seldom what I was able to see and sometimes that was a blessing, but sometimes it was a curse.

You see, when I was younger, I would fall on the concrete. I didn't have the magic grass of the suburbs to hold me up. I fell hard and got bruises and bled. But my city prepared me for love. I knew I would fall and injure myself, especially when I developed a soft spot for you. For anyone. That is just the way that I was composed. God created me to be like that. But, I was taught that it was inevitable that I will fall. I knew that I would. I was just waiting for the timing because I have learned that timing is not something that I can control. So if I must fall, I must stand. I learned both, slowly but surely. I am here starring at you and I am fascinated by how you never left. How you never had enough of me. You were stability. You became unshaken, something I wasn't quite used to with a human.

I woke up. You finally appeared in my dreams, but, as always, I wasn't sure if I was awake or asleep when I wrote this. I don't know if it was my soul, my heart, or my mind that wrote this or if they all were involved in writing this together. I don't think it was all of them since they haven't figured out what gives them all peace when they are placed together so violently. They haven't come to a truce. I don't know. I just know that I didn't get it. Whatever sense that makes.

Letters to Him, 166,

My mind has left me a long time ago. My heart has never abandoned me even though I have broken it plenty of times. I know which one I'd pick. Stability of emotions over reason. Any day. Any night. Any lifetime.

[M.C.]
May 9, 2014
6:01AM

Letters to Him, 167,

And, it was in that moment where I realized that the more I searched, the more lost I became. I realized that I should let it be and somewhere between those crooked lines, I found calmness. That word in itself held so much weight and personal meaning to me because I was always quite close to chaos. The rest looked at the surface only. He and I dug deep into the depths of each other's bones. The rest of them and I could never be together. I'd lose essence of the self. With him, I kept growing. Full.

[M.C.]
May 11, 2014
3:33AM

I went to the place where I felt most safe and where I felt most connected to you. I went by the water just so I could prepare myself for what was coming. I wondered where you were, and I wasn't sure, but I felt you somewhere inside of me. That was enough to keep me going.

Letters to Him, 168,

    I always looked at the sky at night as if it held something so powerful to me. It was almost as if I couldn't breathe without something that it consisted. It was as if a huge chunk of me was up there. All these years, God was trying to show me something: a message that I couldn't understand at first: your religion. He brought you in my life: you who symbolized the moon and the star. You were my universe. I guess that is why I had been obsessed with what the night sky held. You couldn't see them during the day, but at night, the message was revealed. Hidden, like you. You came to me and I was fulfilled. I understood that the world is much greater than it was before. You were my moon and star.

[M.C.]
May 12, 2014
2:03AM

Letters to Him, 169,

You craved my love because you said I reminded you of what life was yet little did you know that I had not known life before you and I care not know what life will be after you.

[M.C.]
May 13, 2014
4:01AM

The time is coming closer...

Letters to Him, 170,

I didn't tell them about you. I swear that your name never left the thin space in between my lips.

Yet, they were still solid witnesses. It was hard for them to be blinded. They saw you swimming deep in my green eyes. You had confused them for the ocean and I allowed them to be your home.

You see, I never opened my mouth when it came to you, but they were solid witnesses, once again. My pen bled for you, every night, until it was drained and it ran out.

[M.C.]
May 15, 2014
1:41AM

Letters to Him, 171,

You see, he was confused. Yes, he might have broken my heart. But the difference is that he sees it as a bad thing. I don't. Maybe our hearts work best when they are all messed up. I think my heart had been concealed in concrete. Maybe a passage of love formed and flowed from the cracks. I never knew that I could love as much as I can now and as freely as I currently do. My heart broke and it bled until the drips of blood led me to the rightful owner of my heart. My heart was trying to free itself and break through its exterior and get to him. So, to this day, I thank you for breaking my heart. It was written in the heavens for that to happen. My heart was never for you. It was always his.

[M.C.]
May 16, 2014
2:19AM

But I guess I didn't realize before, how the struggles were blessings.

All that I knew was the pain. All of this shit, I mean all of it: it was internal damage. I didn't see the blood, but I definitely didn't feel the movement through my bones. They were stiff, completely immobile. No one knew me. I just kept to myself. Each and every day, it was as if a piece of me had died. I never stopped to realize that maybe, just maybe, it wasn't actually damage. I thought to myself, "Was this a form of healing?" But it couldn't be because walking through the dirt, I felt heavy, as if I was just carrying all of this baggage. But, one day, something hit me. I felt myself starting to rise. I learned myself at all different types of low mental states. I was angry, sad, depressed, and numb. They were all waiting for my demise. But, instead of becoming dead, as each day passed, I became art and guess what, it is right now, that I have never felt more alive.

Letters to Him, 172,

    Your lips pressed against my skin, as you tasted the pain that translated into poetry. I was covered in scars, but you had non-hesitantly healed them all and converted them into words for me. You didn't want to alter a thing. You just wanted to know me like every cell in my body knew me. You simply wanted to be the air in my lungs that provided my existence. You reminded me that I was a woman made entirely of symbols. I was not a woman who could be labeled. You beautifully revealed that. And, to this day, you remain in me.

[M.C.]
May 17, 2015
1:19AM

I hope that when my daughter will say that she wants to go on long drives, I will know she is overwhelmed with her inner voices. I hope that when my daughter will say that she is okay when she has bags under her eyes from insomnia, I will notice it. I hope when my daughter will smile 24/7, I will not forget to closely look for the cracks. I hope that when my daughter will be constantly kind and giving, I will not forget to notice how she knows what loss is. I hope that when my daughter will become silent and mute, I will not forget to notice how her pen cries tears and how she buries her face in a notepad. I hope that when my daughter will forget what it is to be trusted, I will not forget to show her that without trust, there is no love: unconditional. And, I hope that when my daughter will cry that she has a father who will show her that her mother has cried, in the same way, while he held her in his arms and wiped away her tears. And to my future daughter, I hope you will know that I was once you, and your father picked me up when I was fallen into pieces. Love exists.

I woke up. God was telling me something. He exists.

Letters to Him, 173,

Don't bother trying to tell me all the flaws that come with him. I know his flaws created him. And don't bother trying to tell me how he is not the richest.

For I know how intrinsically poor the rest of you are. And don't bother trying to tell me that he loved many. For all he did was crave for a love that would reciprocate equally.

I love him for who he is not.

That is enough.

If that even makes sense because it makes perfect sense to me.

[M.C.]
May 20, 2014
6:19AM

They asked me what a perfect night would be like. I was quick to answer and I said: here, with him, writing, while his eyes were fixated on my lips. He would watch at how they stood frozen as they shivered while my pen spills on the paper so that it can somehow reach his soul. It was the only way that I knew how to connect with him. But then, you grabbed my face and intensely looked straight into my eyes. You were so non-hesitant and it was in that moment, you understood. You understood very well. No amount of writing could ever explain the way that my eyes could when yours met mine. I was full. I felt safe. The silent truth stood there firmly. I was yours, utterly and completely. There was no denying that. You saw it. No one else could ever hold the power you had over me.

I woke up. Why was I having all of these dreams and nightmares? It was my fear. They were all my fucking fears. I couldn't overcome them. The time keeps getting closer. I fear time. I do not trust it. I don't trust God fully yet, do I?

Letters to Him, 174,

But, I hide in you every day. Your arms protect me like towers. I will repeat it until I have no more air in me. With you, I am safe. It is true. With you, I am myself.

[M.C.]
May 21, 2014
8:03AM

Letters to Him, 175,

They told me I couldn't find peace. But I did. In a crowded city, I was able to keep a strong mind, but a soft heart. They tried to tear me into pieces. But I rose. I rose higher than a skyscraper. Now, I dance with myself until infinity, while you hold my hand, and dance with me, too. We are two separate bodies in one soul and there will come a day when we will form as one.

[M.C.]
May 22, 2014
5:03AM

Letters to Him, 176,

My soul is like water. Free in the distance, but in chains, when it reaches the shore, for it can never escape the shoreline until there is a natural disaster.

[M.C.]
May 23, 2014
3:09AM

Letters to Him, 177,

You have been patient and have walked by me, through darkness, for an infinite amount of time. And, somewhere within my black soul, you have found the seeds to the red petals that started pouring out. You transformed my soul.

[M.C.]
May 23, 2014
4:10AM

Letters to Him, 178,

You are omnipotent. You have filled me with peace and I surrender my spirituality to you. I whispered to the moon and he allowed me to betray my sleepless nights. You have become my religion.

[M.C.]
May 25, 2014
3:33AM

And that is when my father told me: before you make a decision, whether it is temporary or permanent: clear your mind. Walk amongst the nature, look at the sun, look at the green pigment on the trees, and give all of your worries to them. They observe you and produce all of the oxygen necessary for you to survive, for you to focus on things. My father was rarely wrong, and he wasn't this time, either. All those decisions eventually added up and no decision, whether it be minimal or life changing, was more important than the other. They were links: they were chains that held my life together. They were unconditional chains that held hands and they just wouldn't let go. They refused. No matter what. My father was right. The spark of a clear mind was vital.

I woke up. Fuck! If only I could only understand these signs. But I couldn't. I still was going through an internal battle.

Letters to Him, 179,

Where are you?

[M.C.]
May 29, 2014
3:00AM

I am blind to what they perceive me as. I don't know my appearance at all. I don't see how I look. The mirror can never portray me perfectly and science has proven that. Technically, I never see myself precisely, only others can. So, throughout life, I am left with figuring out who I am internally.

There are different phases, which I go through, in order to understand myself just a little more and more each day. I learn every part of me on my own. The grief, the happiness, the confusion, my faith, and the emotional mysteries are something very personal to me. How contradictory this is! My insides are scars on my soul that no one can ever see unless I expose it to them.

They are my secrets and my gems. How sensitive my insides are compared to my outer being! It should be reversed. I don't bleed for you. I bleed for myself. I know who I am and if I choose to show it to you, that is beautiful. I guess I did choose to show it you. So I guess we are beautiful, together.

Maybe.

June

And I, many times, return to the place where I have walked for days at a time since the young age of four. My father taught me this road. My mother, at times, accompanied us. He taught me to be brave and humble. She taught me to set my sensitive and loving heart free. Now, I treasure it all even though I was sure that my emotions have ruined me many times.

I currently walk, in awe, wondering how the human mind can advance so mysteriously. I feel like I am slowly gathering all of my pieces together and coming to an understanding. I find myself pondering, continuously, as I ask myself, how the human soul can go through such heavy periods of emotions: some full of love and some full of pain. I have discovered my strengths and discovered my weaknesses, while growing daily.

Now, I never knew that solitude could be so sweet. It really could. It can be heavenly if you treat it right and focus on it. I allow myself to cut my heart open. Let it flow into the river, the rapid waters, so that you may learn everything, having knowledge of every part of me.

For you, for this: I bleed, I bleed...

He told her that he would meet her in a conflicting time, in a conflicting world, for a few moments each day. She struggled daily to understand. He said he would return, but hatred started to develop. Her mind consumed her every action. She became weak, fragile, and visibly empty: like a grain of sand.

Everything brought me back to Fire Island, especially as we were getting closer. She would sit at the edge of the water, contemplating who she was. She felt close to anything that took her back to that place. She almost lost herself multiple times. He always saved her. But, her conceptions were flawed. She realized that even the Earth itself was lost at times.

There is a time in the day where the day says goodbye and the night says hello. Humanity called this the sunset. I saw this as a time of confusion, a time of sadness, and a time of departure: all at once.

I felt way too many things all at once. I guess that it was during the day that, many were happy, but the night made me come alive through darkness. There was a time where silence, darkness, and my thoughts consumed me. This was me, for a while, until I realized that the sunset was my reminder to live. It was a reminder that he was still there and that he will always be there to get me through each night. From that moment on, I never doubted that there was a God.

I woke up. I believed again.

Letters to Him, 180,

It is a little too often that people think that it means nothing to be empty. They categorize empty with the word nothing. It is a synonym. And maybe it does, in fact, mean nothing to some who don't care to search deep within their souls. But, there are those people who feel with their whole soul. There are those who don't know how to feel any other way. I look back, and I realize that I used to feel way too much. I felt everything too deeply. There are still disbursements where I still feel a little too much, but never as much as I used to. Still, I think the beauty has not been stolen. I used to fear the time where I would be so empty that I felt nothing. I was like that for a long time. I felt numb to everything, but him. Then, when he didn't reciprocate, it was like my soul was murdered. Few understood me; I don't think anyone did. But guess what? I have become so emptied that I have awakened last night. I feel like I have emptied everything that has harmed me and I have more room to be filled again than I ever had. Every time you leave my soul, my body naturally produces more space to accept you again.

[M.C.]
June 2, 2014
6:01AM

Letters to Him, 181,

The moon is the most loyal companion if you really think about it. Our souls were almost as loyal because, at times, you even had the ability to leave my soul even though you lived here. The moon has yet to leave my side. It is always there picking apart and analyzing every part of me: the physical and the spiritual. It watches me in awe, as I sometimes try to seduce it with my strength.

Sometimes, it watches me in despair, as I try to harm it with my weaknesses. The moon understands what it is like to be both human and immortal. It has imperfections: it stands alone with no company. It stands not sure of what tomorrow will bring.

It is sometimes ugly because it is always changing. But, it is also immortal because no matter how dark the day may be, it never forgets to shine bright and bring peace into our lives. No matter how much the moon may change, it never forgets to go back to who it was once in a while. Tonight, the moon decided to be full. And tonight, it went back to its original state. By this, it decided to be strong and gather all of its pieces up together, to remind us that we, as humans, can do it too. We are forever one soul if we choose to be. We always go back to our natural state, and at the core of you, is I.

[M.C.]
June 3, 2014
2:19AM

I didn't want you to arrive at a time when I didn't know myself well. Now, that I am slowly gaining my faith in God back, whoever He is and wherever He is, I am starting to think that it is possible that everything has happened for a reason even though they try to make you think otherwise. They try to form your thoughts and make you think like them. They try to make you not believe in love. They try, they really, really do, but I didn't let them succeed. That would mean that I would have to allow them to have control over my heart, my soul, my body, and my mind. I would never allow that. I could never allow that. For that reason alone, for the first time in a long time, I am sure that you will exist. You have to. There was simply no other way. Time kept coming closer and closer. You kept coming closer and closer. They can say otherwise, but you will be here. Soon.

Letters to Him, 182,

I am coming closer to you. I hope that when I arrive, you have not completely altered your being from your soul. I hope you didn't run from it. I hope you followed it to the point where it has destroyed you so many times that you had to choice, but to learn and rebuild yourself plenty of times over and over again.

[M.C.]
June 4, 2014
3:00AM

Letters to Him, 183,

They said that his eyes were ordinary because they didn't resemble the ocean. To them, they were brown and dull. But, I saw my soul whenever I looked into them. I found depths that the ocean itself didn't possess. So, no, they didn't resemble the ocean, they resembled something much, much greater. Something that I, myself, could never put into words.

[M.C.]
June 6, 2014
2:05AM

Tonight, my mother and I had a conversation. It wasn't much, but I felt it. She usually talks to me, and although I hear her, I never listen.

Not that I didn't want to, because I had such a deep love for my mother, but because listening to someone consists of taking everything they are saying in.

She told me, "You're getting there, Merzi."

This was all that kept replaying inside of my mind all day. I knew that I was getting there.

Everything was connecting and I realized that some higher power gave me the strength to not give up. I was getting stronger by the day, can't you tell?

Letters to Him, 184,

She fell in love with the escape into a world where she isolated herself. She was a runaway. She became so lost in words that they made love to her mind for hours at a time. And, it was those exact moments that he dreaded. He feared that those words had known her more intimately than he had ever been able to understand her. She remained a mystery. Yet had he known that every time he breathed, he allowed her pen to flow onto the paper. Without him, her words would be without substance.

[M.C.]
June 7, 2014
1:01AM

I kept writing although I feared that the removal of the pain would steal my talent.

I feared a lot, didn't I?

"Stop it with the rhetorical questions, Merzi."

Some events triggered my mind and they made me want to transfer my thoughts onto paper again. You know it happens, and sometimes, too often. There are times when I am filled with the gift of writing, but, there are other times, that completely steal the writing away from my soul. There are times that I cannot write at all. What an unforgiving thief such a force could be.

It is like an outside force interrupts me in the midst of my daily movements. It is a curse and a blessing because my peace, frequently, becomes broken. Today is Monday and, too often, the beginning of a new week trembles people. Too often, it makes them anxious and inattentive. I woke up feeling this way, too. In case you ever feel like this, just know that you are not alone.

I had him inside of my soul and he interrupted me, again. He woke my inner soul up and I felt alive. Signs are everywhere. I mean it. They are literally everywhere. You just have to follow your soul and, sometimes, let your reason overcome your emotions just the right amount. Blessings will lead me to you. It is destiny. It was never a plan that I could create or control. I was starting to believe this.

There were times where I reverted back because I wasn't completely okay yet. I hope that you do not think that everything is okay now just because I seem to be moving along through life decently. I am still hurting deep inside, but I realized that I am just a human who feels every single emotion too much, as if you couldn't tell already. It just took me time to learn how to deal with some things. We all go through phases. I don't think I did because I always remained, but I learned to survive with it. That was the only difference. At times, I did revert back, though.

Life just seems a little different now. I guess that is the best way to describe it. Just, different. I feel numb, but it is in those moments that I also feel alive. You taught me to live and because of this, too often, I pause and think of you. You never leave my mind and you most definitely will not leave my soul. I still feel as if you are here. It feels as if your body has never left earth. Your footprints have left marks on the ground, leaving roots that will grow into beautiful generations. But although there is still pain, acceptance brings me inner peace. You are here, through me. And, perhaps, this is how I know God. Perhaps, this is how you can feel Him even though he is not physically here. What a liberating feeling it is to know that you are here even though you are not in sight. I love you all the way from earth to heaven.

I woke up. God was talking to me again. The only difference is that, this time, I wasn't ignoring Him. I was listening. I paid attention to His signs. He taught me He was here, but that I could do it myself. He taught me not to depend on Him. I felt my brother's soul inside of me. That was unconditional love. Through love, I gained strength. Always. I learned that even the pain that came with it was worth it.

Letters to Him, 185,

I looked at him and I could just tell. It was like my gut was yelling at me so that I would notice him. And I did. I saw everything. There was a burden that was holding him down. It was weighing on him so heavily. It was heavier than any heavy metal would actually feel like on his shoulders. I feel his story without even laying a finger on him.

I could just sit across from him and read his mind. It was insane. It was like I had already felt everything that he felt, but twice as worse. It was like he just wants to burst and tell this story to everyone he meets just to see if he will connect with something. He searched everywhere and anywhere to see if anyone would get him. He lives with hopes that someone will have a similar story, with hopes that someone can help him piece him together. He wants to show me who he was, how he grew up, and everything about his family.

That is what I see when I look in his eyes. He is completely lost and the fact that he can't be raw and open: I can tell that it is a burden to him. Until I hear it, it is like we can't even start yet. But still, it is like I feel every part of him. It is the most powerful feeling that I have ever felt. It was surely something stronger than love.

[M.C.]
June 7, 2014
8:05AM

Letters to Him, 186,

When it came to him, it was never hard to explain and I will repeat it until the air in my lungs dry out. I feel most comfortable with that man. He not only sees me, but he sees through me. He cut through impossibility. He knows me, not only physically, but mentally. He knows my cells and everything that composes me: who I was and who I am. He even knows who I will be. As long as he knows himself and his own soul, he will forever know me. With anyone else, it was so terribly unnatural. With him, it is quite freeing and powerful.

[M.C.]
June 8, 2014
4:01AM

Letters to Him, 187,

Promise me that you leaving will not be familiar to me. Promise me that even if you leave, you will return to me, even if it takes as long as the next life. I promise that I will search for you in whatever decade my soul resides. I promise that destiny will bring me to you in the next life if not in this one. The age does not matter. I can be 16, 22, 35, 60 or whatever time frame fate chooses to give us a chance. And, if destiny is stolen from us or if it loses itself, please promise me that you will still search for me. Look for me everywhere, even in the places that are least expected and even when it is hardest for you to do so. Even if the sun has become annihilated and all that is known to everyone is darkness: until the end of time. This is what I mean when I say that we are infinite.

[M.C.]
June 9, 2014
1:23AM

I sit here, with some people, but I still feel like no one is around me because I am so sucked into my feelings. No one is really able to feel like I do.

Not an ounce of alcohol has to touch the tip of my tongue in order for me to turn numb. Your name runs deeper than that. You cannot be forgotten. To forget you is to forget the self.

You flow through my blood, reaching every part of my body: faster than the speed of light. It is something that no scientific measure can explain. You ignite every desire as if you were made out of fire. Perhaps your soul was composed of this. Your love has the power to calculate my every step, containing toxins strong enough to paralyze my movements. While everyone is trying to drink his or her lover away with outer substances, I am here, so perfectly sober yet so imperfectly still.

I miss you.

Letters to Him, 188,

Have you arrived yet?

[M.C.]
June 9, 2014
3:00AM

Sometimes, the world still gets a little too much for me. It becomes a little too consuming. And, sometimes, the only thing I need is escape and to get away for a while in order for my heart and my mind to clear and filter itself. So, if he searches, tell him to find me in the place where the essence of innocence still rests for me.

There, I can retrace all of my steps that have led me to my growth: the very core of who I am. I search for a place where no weights are placed on the shoulders. I search for a place where I go to free my soul. I search for a place that knows no pride. I search for a place that knows no ego. I search for a place that only knows peace and love. I search for complete freedom. I think that everyone has one of those "hiding spots." At least I hope that they do and if he is able to find me there: let it be beautiful.

Love finds you even when you hide away from it.

He will exist.

July

Sometimes, I think about who we are and my soul shakes a little. I become scared. I think about what the individual human is made of. The majority of us spend so much time on calculation: it almost goes against who we are. It goes against our essence, our soul.

Have we become robot-like? This is us, in our ugliest state. It is in this where we are locked and in chains, like Rousseau had firmly believed. We look at our every movement; we have become nothing but mechanical. We create a prison for ourselves, for our souls, and for our minds. Maybe this is what they spoke about when they said that we sell our souls to the devil.

Maybe it is in our daily actions that this comes to light. Do you ever catch yourself lost? Is there ever that moment where you think: I don't belong here? Maybe, just maybe, at that moment, our souls are trying to tell us something: our composition.

I still went by the water in anticipation of the return in August...

Letters to Him, 189,

They were like two bodies of water, but so different. The first, well, he, resembled a lake. My whole body was submerged, but the water stayed calm around my skin: only getting to know how my surface was like, never getting inside to really find out who I was. But the second, yes, the second, was quite rare. He was like the ocean: full of waves. I stood near him as the waves violently pressed against my skin. He was unstoppable until he reached my inner core, breaking through every skin wall that I had built. One after another, the waves broke down all of the cell walls that covered my skin. If I were to choose the first "him," I might love comfortably, but my soul would never reach its full potential. Now, if I love the second, "him," who resembled the ocean, he would reach a level that no other man could have reached with me. His waves never halted until they completely destroyed my exterior, but it calmed my interior, completely.

[M.C.]
July 2, 2014
1:01AM

As the days go by, I am finding that I feel more alive. During the daytime, many things seems so perfect to some people, and sometimes, this instills fear inside of me. I am quite the thinker, as you can all already tell, and I couldn't help but think that you had failed to see the real me. I just wish that you could actually stay forever when you arrive, if you even arrive. I want you to be strong enough to know that my imperfections will appear at night. When everyone leaves and isolation hits, I am alone with my own soul. That is when I am most raw. This is where I am most free. I am who I am at 3AM.

Letters to Him, 190,

They told me that my heart only feels. They told me that it does nothing else except produce feelings. What a disaster that would be! I never believed them. Did you really find me to be that naive? I always knew that my heart was much more than that. If you listen carefully, it speaks louder than your mind. I swear.

[M.C.]
July 3, 2014
3:03AM

Letters to Him, 191,

Let me breathe for a moment, these lungs have been tired for too long. Give my mind a rest, my heart would like to speak without uttering a word. And it does. There are goose bumps on my skin and this is living and physical proof that you still live inside of me, somewhere within. You always will.

[M.C.]
July 4, 2014
9:07PM

Letters to Him, 192,

I told him to cut me open and tear me apart. Please break my walls down, even the roughest edges. Please get into my heart and not only my mind. It would only be then where he would understand me completely. Only then, would he be comfortable in knowing that his name flows through my veins. I bleed for you and it will run through generations. Infinite. Just like I always had repeated.

[M.C.]
July 5, 2014
12:05AM

I thought I had felt everything that was left to feel. I thought my soul was too full and that it didn't have room for anything or anyone else. I thought my mind was already full with too many memories. I thought that my shoulders felt too heavy. I thought that my heart couldn't feel love anymore.

But then your eyes met mine.

I woke up. Here I was again. I was at the same spot where I wrote for the longest of days. I am at the same spot where my soul bled for you for many nights that I haven't slept. My bed is filled with my mind's thoughts of you. I have created you into my surroundings somehow. You live in the air that I breathe. It gives me oxygen. I had too much anxiety today because the time was getting closer. I was unsure if I was ready to give up or meet you. How about if you turn out to be the opposite of what I had expected? What then? Will I still love you? Will you love me? I don't know. I can't tell the future.

"Shut the fuck up Merzi." I laughed. I still had it. My mind was still talking to me. I was still fucking insane.

Letters to Him, 193,

But the other one. I hope you never had or will have to go through this. The other one swallowed my soul and spit it out naked. That one almost left me with no soul. But he, he, rapidly took those bones and he made a masterpiece of whatever was left of me. He reconstructed my human body all over again. Before, I was a robot. He, yes he, turned me back into my childhood state: a human.

[M.C.]
July 7, 2014
7:07AM

Letters to Him, 194,

Some looked away. Some were frightened by me. Some intimidated. Some uninterested. But he, he couldn't take his eyes off of me. And, I couldn't understand why and maybe that is why I pushed him away.

Him: the way that he explained me was mesmerizing. He made my most simple, ordinary movements, sound as if I breathed out little masterpieces every single time I spoke. He loved me best when my soul was completely naked. To be specific, he loved me most at night, because he knew that it was the time that I needed it most. He knew I needed it most because my soul reflected the moon at that time. And I couldn't thank him enough for that. I really couldn't.

[M.C.]
July 9, 2014
2:07AM

Letters to Him, 195,

My soul has run wild. Yet it is the master of its own fate. Free yet self-controlled. A beautiful paradox.

[M.C.]
July 10, 2014
4:03AM

Letters to Him, 196,

And, sometimes, your hands feel like they are crippling.
And, sometimes, your mind feels weak.
And, sometimes, your feet feel as if they have no more movements.
And, sometimes, your skin feels a little too thin.
And, sometimes, your eyes lose vision.
And, sometimes, taste becomes a little too bitter.
And, sometimes, your ears hear thoughts that are nonexistent.
But through this, although your heart may feel silent, it still beats.
And, **SOMETIMES** this makes you **ALIVE**.

[M.C.]
July 11, 2014
5:07AM

And the sad thing is: I close my eyes, but it does not go away. Usually, people get peace, especially at night. They were normal. I was odd. I was strange. It was still just me in a world, all alone. I closed my eyes to escape reality, just for a second, but it wouldn't go away. It crept up on me even in my dreams. That was probably the worst. I still had fear inside of me. The days were coming too soon and I didn't know what to do. I waited.

Letters to Him, 197,

Everything may seem disconnected. This is possible. But, as each day passes, I am starting to trust fate more. You will exist, right?

[M.C.]
July 12, 2014
3:00AM

I felt it way too much. It was a little too unmoving. It felt like I could not make it out alive. The way he breathed made it a little difficult to say goodbye. The way that I moved was in complete sync with the rhythm of his heart. Our souls moved as one. He breathed me to life and allowed me to dance freely, igniting every part of me as if I were a candle. He did this well by just being alive. But, I knew I had to say goodbye and I had to accept the consequences. I feared nothing. I just felt myself become unharmonious and my steps became a little too bitter. Without you, my steps were unbalanced. I was not even afraid of death anymore. The only time I feared death was when I thought that our goodbye might transfer into the afterlife. I was scared that I wouldn't meet you in the afterlife. Then what?

The strange thing was that he could not see me when I was here. I turned invisible. But now, that I am one with the wind, he sees me everywhere. I blow through his soul...

I woke up. It was almost time. These were the signs. I just could not figure my destiny out. I kept trying, but it just wouldn't come to me. How unfair life can be at times. I was filled with fear now more than ever.

God, please help! I think that this is the first time that I have asked for your help in a while. I think I finally need you.

Letters to Him, 198,

He looked at her as she lay there on the cold cement, in the pouring rain, hoping that the rain would wash him away from her. He feared that he would only hurt her. For the first time, she felt him melt away. She felt him come off of her skin, off of her soul, like the candle that would run out, if lit. We were scared to light it for the fear that the wax will run out. And, he would always tell me "it would always run out, love." So now I lay here, in the rain, and I no longer fear the thunder. The candle may have run out, but I told him that he has permanently lit a fire in my soul and I dared him to come and see that no matter how much the rain tries to set it out: it wouldn't dare try. Even the forces of the universe feared him.

[M.C.]
July 13, 2014
6:03AM

Letters to Him, 199,

He loved me for the way I made him feel alive yet
he was my reason for existence.

[M.C.]
July 14, 2014
2:05AM

Letters to Him, 200,

He said that I reminded him of the rain. I was washing him away from all of his sins. With me, he was born again. He became new. I was his last hope. I wouldn't dare let him down.

[M.C.]
July 15, 2014
3:09AM

Letters to Him, 201,

I would walk through hell and live there. I would breathe its dusty air if it meant his spiritual return. A part of me will never go to heaven if he is in hell.

[M.C.]
July 16, 2014
1:53AM

I was supposed to be a butterfly, but I was that injured caterpillar whose wings did not want to spread. I was stuck inside of my own self. But then I awoke and I realized that I had all this power. I became alive. Time is near. Once again, I loved and hated these small realizations.

Letters to Him, 202,

Before he was even born, God placed her in his heart. He told him that there will be mental wars, many broken places, hurt, and bloodshed. But, he will know very well when he finds her: she is his peace.

I laughed again. God always found a way to tell me His secrets. This time, it was through my pen.

[M.C.]
July 17, 2014
3:47AM

Letters to Him, 203,

I was certain of nothing except for him. I knew him a little too well, so well, that my mind memorized every cell in his body. The way he moved brought me to life. I knew him so well that my heart felt his sadness and his joy. I knew him a little too well, so well that it was damaging to the self. You see, I knew him, but he didn't know me. Or did you? I feared this.

[M.C.]
July 18, 2014
12:39AM

I guess I will let you in on the secret of what I almost did tonight.

I had about **583** letters for you up until this date. I told you earlier that I actually hid some from you and will not include them in here because they were too much for you to see. They went against you and I feared that they were not meant for your eyes. They were meant only for mine. They were meant to make me better so that we could be individuals before we met each other. We could understand and be ourselves fully. So, I tore them apart and I let them burn. I closed my eyes to escape reality just for a second or a brief moment, but it these thoughts would not go away. The memories of those letters ran after me. You crept up on me, even in my dreams. Here, I learned my transition of trust from the physical into the emotional. I fell in love with the unseen. That was probably the worst. I fell in love with something I was not sure existed, you. You see, **mind** is a funny thing, but the **heart** gets whatever it wants. **Believe me.**

Fuck. The time is here.

August

...I sit here staring out into the water. There is nothing but open space everywhere. The way that the waves move may hypnotize me because everything is coming out of me and spilling onto this paper. I don't think I know you yet, but I wonder if you see the moon the way I do.

I wonder if you look at the moon with fear and a bit of awe. I wonder if each time you glance at the moon and then look down at the water, you feel peace. I wonder if in that one second everything becomes okay for you, as it becomes for me. I wonder if you give the moon complete power over you for that little while. I wonder if your heart whispers all of your problems to the water, hoping the waves will take them away from you, as I do.

I wonder if you look at people wondering that they need to change the way they love. I wonder if you look at people and you feel that they need to change the way that they maintain their loyalty. I wonder if you feel the need to know about people's very core. I chose to be alone at night so I can get to know myself a little better and I wonder if you did the same, too.

You are what I wanted. You were always what I had wanted and to this day, this scares me. I don't know if you will exist at all because I thought that this year would bring me greater closure than I currently have. I don't know if you will come find me. I don't know if a greater power will bring you to me. I don't know if we will cross each other's paths. I guess the uncertainty of everything is making me lose hope, but, at the same time, the certainty that my heart has cannot be defeated. It is not in me to let my heart lose and let my mind win. I was determined to force them to come to peace. He will exist. I am the female version of him.

I still write just so I can try to find you.

Letters to Him, 204,

My heart survives on feelings. He knows who I am so well that his mind enters mine without me even knowing him. I close my eyes and try to feel you somewhere within me. I call this euphoria.

[M.C.]
August 3, 2014
3:00AM

I survived off of this. Everything about this place was raw. My emotions were raw. Everything felt like I had it at my reach and the crazy thing was that my nightmares disappeared now that I was here. It was strange, though, because I thought that I would reach complete peace now that I was here. I didn't. I was starting to think that my mind was playing tricks on me, but I still couldn't fully believe it. I would hate myself if I made myself believe something that wasn't real. I believed in you so much that I stole my own reality. I stole my own mind. "Merzi, Shut up!" I swear that my mind had the potential to kill me. I just wanted to walk around Fire Island and feel, but it was so hard to even feel anything. I wasn't sure about how I was feeling and I wasn't sure about what I would do.

Letters to Him, 205,

    I am always chasing all of the million things that I want and those things, whatever they may be, when I run and catch up to them, so beautifully just stop, and walk right by my side. This is where I got the will to find you. There is a certain kind of peace in grasping what you want. And, you have always been my peace.

[M.C.]
August 3, 2014
3:29AM

Letters to Him, 206,

I guess I am a little "too human." I am composed of imperfections, but I have a supernatural force in me and it is quite strange. There are times when I am so confused because I just don't know where it came from. I have yet to find its origin and even understand it fully. I do not know its source. I understand too well what it is that humanity lacks and although I am aware, I cannot change it. I really cannot because I am only human. We can never perfect ourselves even if we are aware of what it is that we lack and need. And this is terrible because. for love, I am a perfectionist. This is the tragedy of all love.

[M.C.]
August 3, 2014
3:39AM

I hate you so much that my skin gets goose bumps at the thought of you steadying my hand. I hate you so much that my eyes become blind every single time I see you. I hate you so much that my lips shiver every time I speak of anything that reminds me of you. I hate you so much that my thoughts drown themselves into the depth of my blood cells. I hate you so much that my ears become a little too deaf every single time someone mentions you. I hate you so much that I want to destroy every single cologne that has ever resembled your smell. I hate you so much that I want to reword every lyric that brings you back to the depths of my soul.

I woke up. I thought that I would finally stop having nightmares now that I was back in Fire Island, but they just didn't go away. They came back. I go to rub my eyes, but the grains of sand spread all over my face and almost went into my eyes. I guess that I fell asleep on the beach again. "Merzi! Calm Down!" My mind could not leave me alone. I finally stopped to listen to what my heart had to say. I had a habit of listening to my mind so much that I would silence my heart. My actions were not fair.

But, after all of that, I realized that I love you a little too much, so much, that I have allowed you to consume me, fully.

Letters to Him, 207,

Just know that no matter how long it will take, I believe that the souls that are meant to be together, will be together. I believe that God has written everything, but I believe that this is too simple. This is just too easy. If I believed that, then it would mean that I would also believe that God thinks that we are too weak. It would mean that God has no trust in us at all. So, I do not fully believe this even though there are times when I heavily do. What I do believe is that He trusts us enough in order to give us the will power to go after the love that we want. In a way, He lets us choose. I fear that I will not find someone who has the same definition of love as I do because I seem to not fit in anywhere. I seem to be alone so much that it is starting to take a toll on me. It is true that we all have so many different definitions, but on all of these years on Earth, I have yet to find a love that matches mine. I have yet to find someone who can love as strongly as I do. I have yet to find someone strong enough. My love tends to be so strong that it usually kills many souls before they even have the chance to love me back. Please, do not misunderstand me. I have not lost faith in you. I still believe that you will exist. You have to exist because one soul is not enough to deal with this world. I believe that another stronger soul is needed in order to give us all the power to love. I have yet to meet everyone in this world, so I cannot say that the love that I am capable of does not exist... I guess...I guess... I don't know. What I do know is that he will exist.

[M.C.]
August 4, 2014
3:00AM

Letters to Him, 208,

And, your legacy will stay. You are forever. You are infinite. You are immortal. I have constantly written about you, not just with the pen and paper, but my breath has written your name in the air. You are in my soul and you have moved with me. Everywhere that I have went, you have followed, even if I could not see. Your body may perish, but your soul will live on earth eternally. He will exist.

[M.C.]
August 5, 2014
3:01AM

He keeps saying he is done and that he wants to escape this hell, but he is lying to himself. He is internally bleeding, without stopping to look at life, without perceiving reality, without even giving his mind or soul a bit of a rest. Maybe, if he breathes a little, his feet will start to slowly move: one by one, and he will escape this broken tune that the world has created for him. Maybe the peaceful summer nights have created storms for him and maybe it feels as if there is no escape left. Maybe every corner feels as if it is metal. Maybe he can't carve his way out. His soul is crying. It is so fearful and filled with doubt. Maybe, if he starts to write on those walls, he can create beauty and make it his home. Maybe it is not so bad after all. Just maybe, if he starts to look at life with a different vision, maybe if he stops wanting to roam, maybe then, he will feel free. Maybe, only then will God hear his plea.

I woke up. I could have sworn that he lives inside of me.

Looking at the waves crash into the sand, from time to time, day by day, I stop and think, what a breath of fresh air it is to remember that we are just human. We create our own little worlds and we get lost in them. We constantly get trapped in our thoughts. Maybe, as a whole population, that is our biggest flaw, let alone as individuals. We forget that we are part of a bigger world yet we crave isolation so deeply. Maybe this is my tragedy. Maybe you were my tragedy. "Shut up Merzi!" There goes my mind once again. It could never catch up to my heart…

Letters to Him, 209,

What a tragedy it would have been had I allowed one person to change my whole perception into something negative, make me bitter, and make me lose love. I would have never met you.

[M.C.]
August 6, 2014
3:33AM

I stared out into the ocean at Fire Island as I wrote this...

Letters to Him, 210,

All she needs is for the universe to align,
Yet, her soul went missing.
To the world's surprise, it has escaped and hid itself on the moon's surface.
And, if you were to ever look for her, if you were to ever seek her spirit, do not look for perfection for you will never find her.
Look for her in the depths of chaos. Look everywhere that is invisible. She is hidden away written on the skin of the wind...

[M.C.]
August 6, 2014
3:39AM

I looked at my surroundings and everything felt smaller than when I had previously seen it. I used to sit on the sand in this exact same spot and feel so small compared to everything else. But, maybe, this is what happens when you learn more about yourself. Everything that I had once known becomes small compared to who I am now. But, it is not like me to forget it.

Perhaps, it is just because I knew it at a time when I didn't really know myself. Maybe, when I stepped out of my comfort zone, I looked back at my comfort zone and I saw that it wasn't bigger than me. I am bigger than anything that tries to defeat me...

Fate. It often spoke louder than anything else. It spoke louder than words and even louder than actions. I thought about this as my world completely stopped. "How did you end up here?" I asked myself this question many times. "How was I at the same spot as you were?" I asked myself once again.

I swore back to heaven and earth about a million times that I would never see you again. I thought that I had no desire to and I had no craving to ever make peace with your eyes. I wanted you gone, gone, like the wind. But, I guess I learned that even wind couldn't control fate. I guess nothing could move fate. Nothing could move what was destined. Nothing could change it and nothing could alter it.

I thought about all of this as your eyes finally caught mine while I was sitting on the beach, burying my face in my notebook, with my pen in my right hand. My heart kept beating louder and I felt my whole body paralyze. I saw you, there you were. It was as if God had breathed fate onto earth. You were meant to be there at that moment. And I, well I, was like a molecule. At that moment, my world had turned into disorder.

I didn't wake up. I was awake. My dreams were turning into reality. The only difference was that you weren't here yet.

Letters to Him, 211,

I have always feared others leaving, so much, that I became fearful to the point where I resulted into a recluse. I conquered my fear, but I think that was my greatest downfall. I feared it so much that I began to analyze it. I began to analyze every detail of it. Instead of conquering my fear, I turned into my fear. I became my fear. I kept leaving and I had no idea how to stop.

[M.C.]
August 7, 2014
3:00AM

These thoughts keep stabbing their way into my mind. I say stabbing because I try to create metal barriers so they cannot enter, but it is nearly impossible. There are times where I fear that I still do not know who I am. There are times when I sit here, on the sand of Fire Island, starring out into the ocean and I do not know what I am made up of.

There are times when I fear that I will never know myself to the point where I am comfortable allowing you to know me. I know myself better than I knew myself last year, but, still, I fear that I am only made up of theories. I fear that I have lost touch of the physical side of me. I exist through thoughts, but I fear that you will never know me because I fear that a person like me will never cross your mind. And, if I do not exist in your thoughts, I could never exist in the physical. I am alive because of my mind. Ironically, because most believed my mind was beautiful yet it was the same exact thing that was killing me.

I was convinced that my mind could save me, but I wasn't sure how. I wasn't sure how to convert you from my thoughts and make you a reality. I didn't know. I kept trying to know, but the results were never how I wanted them to be. Then again, I thought of destiny. And, I thought of how I couldn't control destiny. I wasn't the one with the power even though I was the one who had the will. I could only control things to a certain extent. I could only create to a certain extent. I still believe that Fire Island is my soul's home.

I still believe in you.

Letters to Him, 212,

    If you ever doubt your existence, even if it is for a split second, I hope you remember that someone lives for you. My soul becomes alive only because you are alive.

[M.C.]
August 7, 2014
3:03AM

Letters to Him, 213,

I think I fell in love with you when you showed me your pain. I admired the way your character never changed although many tried to steal bits and pieces of you. Instead of changing, your heart kept growing. You had a healing power. You had the power to heal, not only me, but also everyone who has ever known pain.

[M.C.]
August 7, 2014
3:11AM

Letters to Him, 214,

You were my protector. So, when you left, you left me in a chaotic world. You left me in a place where my wounds were completely opened. You were not there to help me heal them. I hate you for that.

[M.C.]
August 7, 2014
3:17AM

"Merzi, I can't believe it has been a year and you still believe that he exists even though he has only appeared in your mind." I smiled. That was my mind talking. I don't pay attention to that anymore. I had perfected the ability to turn my thoughts off now. I listened, but my thoughts couldn't affect me. I was learning to control my mind and follow my heart more and more every day. It was quite beautiful, if you asked me.

Letters to Him, 215,

You always told me that I was you. You said we were the same. You lied. I would have never thought of leaving your side, but you thought of leaving mine. You allowed my fear to consume me and now all I am left with are my bones. I feel nothing emotionally.

[M.C.]
August 7, 2014
3:27AM

"Merzi, Shut the fuck up. He doesn't exist yet. Your mind is crazy." I still wasn't listening to my mind, though. I kept following my heart. It wouldn't fail me contrary what the others believed.

Letters to Him, 216,

There is nothing I hold closer to me than you. We might not have spoken, but your name has grown roots deep inside of my blood, your memory has traveled through my bones, and it has reached its way to my heart, causing irreparable cracks until your return. This is immortality, but I have remained human. You have remained a God.

[M.C.]
August 7, 2014
3:31AM

Letters to Him, 217,

You think that you have cursed that man because you think that I will never look at him the way that I have looked at you. You think that you have taken everything away from me. You think that I will never trust him the way that I have trusted you. You think that I will never love him the way that I have loved you. You have never been more right. I will look at him with greater peace. I will trust him with every fiber in my being, and I will love him more. I will love him unconditionally and he will do the same to me.

[M.C.]
August 7, 2014
3:33AM

Staring at the ocean, once again, my days were going by fairly quickly. The reason that I decided to go to Fire Island alone was so that I could get to know myself even better. Few knew how much this meant to me. I kept writing so that I could find my peace before he would arrive.

I bottled so much inside of me that I was surprised to see how many different emotions showed up when the ink hit the paper. It was my IV and it was keeping me alive. I thought that you were the IV that has bandaged my wounds. And you did, but you did it too beautifully.

We were each other's peace. I am just confused about the exact moment that we declared this emotional war that seems like it will never end. I want, with my entire being, to go back to that exact moment and change it. I am sorry if it was, in any way, my fault. This is just a little too much to deal with.

And, I know that I am strong, but ever since your eyes have met mine, you have been the only weakness that I have known. I guess I was confused because I still wasn't sure if you existed, but my heart was determined that you will exist. And, you know, my heart was never wrong.

Maybe, just maybe, my heart persuaded my mind.

Letters to Him, 218,

He extinguished the strongest flame that was in my heart. I could never love anyone the same way that I had loved him.

[M.C.]
August 8, 2014
3:23AM

You became a part of my being. If you were to ever leave, if these letters were to ever end and you were to never appear, I would not know what to do with myself. I was afraid that I wouldn't know what to do with my mind. I was afraid that I wouldn't know what to do with my heart. At least in my writings, he existed.

Letters to Him, 219,

I miss you like the day craves the night, but the light never quite gets to encounter the darkness. They say that opposites attract, but the night and the day are forever separate. They can't live with or without the other. They are not meant to be together. This was the kind of destiny that I would always talk about...

[M.C.]
August 8, 2014
3:33AM

Letters to Him, 220,

How can they say there is beauty in missing someone when I feel as if I lose a part of myself, without you, with each second that passes by?

[M.C.]
August 8, 2014
3:53AM

Letters to Him, 221,

I was so full and I saw that he was empty. He was completely depleted. I gave him all of me just so that he could become a better man. Love is wanting the other to have happiness even if it means giving up yours, right?

[M.C.]
August 9, 2014
3:00AM

Letters to Him, 222,

You made leaving so beautiful that I was in a constant search for traces of you, everywhere, in everything and in everyone...
You made the most ugly things beautiful, for me.

[M.C.]
August 9, 2014
3:03AM

Even though I kept feeling these conflicting emotions, I kept learning more and more about myself with each day that passed by in Fire Island. I kept learning that love was the most important thing to me. Without love, not just of Him, but also of the self, I did not have anything. For some, money makes them happy. For some, success makes them happy. For some, reputation makes them happy. But, for me, I do not think that I could ever be full without love. I do not think that I, as a human, would feel complete. I would always feel as if something were missing.

Trust is a great component of love for me. So, I went by the water, in order to try to trust the waves of the ocean once again. I kept trying to regain the innocence I had lost when I had become paralyzed to the world. I created this anxiety within myself that I didn't really know how to fix.

I began trusting the inside of me too much—so much that I began to not know what trust was when it came to the outside world. I couldn't trust nature, but if I had believed in destiny as much as I really did, shouldn't I believe in nature? Shouldn't I trust it? If I loved the water as much as I said I did, shouldn't I trust it? How could I tell my secrets to something and find peace in something that I could not fully trust? These were all the questions that my mind kept pressing my heart about.

My mind wouldn't leave my heart alone. It wouldn't give my heart peace until it understood every little detail. These are the tragedies of a human. We want to understand everything and we can't just trust and feel. Our experiences shape us into something calculated. They shape us into something that we weren't meant to be. But, then again, here goes my mind, trying to analyze what I just said.

"Merzi, what about destiny? How about if we were meant to go through these experiences to shape who we are?" I don't know anymore. I never knew. Once again, all I know is that he will exist.

Letters to him, 223,

You called me your angel and I looked at you as if you were a type of God. I surrendered all my power to you, but you ignored how heavily you have destroyed my wings. I do not know if I have any more innocence left inside of me to ever be your angel again.

[M.C.]
August 9, 2014
3:13AM

Letters to Him, 224,

Nothing in the world feels as good as the one you love opening the inner core of your soul, carefully, just so they can know how beautiful you really are. There will be those who will never love you unconditionally and will enter and try to take pieces of your soul, but they will fail because no one can take something that belongs to you. But, the man who will love you unconditionally will memorize your soul and carefully put you back together without leaving a trail of pain. When you come across this man, keep him forever. Do not let him go.

[M.C.]
August 9, 2014
3:23AM

Letters to Him, 225,

You have such beautiful outer layers, but the inside of you is so horrifying ugly that you have had the capability of spraying out illusions, which you have blinded yourself to, as well. You are worse than poison. Even poison knows its own effects. Even poison knows that it can kill people. You killed my soul without even knowing.

[M.C.]
August 9, 2014
3:47AM

"Merzi, stop writing as if you hate him for not coming on time. You don't." See, my heart accepted this and didn't block it from my mind. It was convenient. I told you that I became a pro at blocking out thoughts that I did not want to accept, but keeping the thoughts that I did.

Letters to Him, 226,

   I fear that I will watch your eyes get bitter by the second. I fear that you will look at me as if I held your world and, then, out of nowhere, you will look at me as if I was your version of hell. I fear that you will not see the angel in me and try to create me into a devil...

[M.C.]
August 9, 2014
3:49AM

Letters to Him, 227,

There are no other measurements of who a human really is except for the heart. It is in the heart that makes us different. It is the heart that makes us not equal. It is in the love that we hold that we are not all equal. That is the only way to measure a man. That is the only way that I will measure you.

[M.C.]
August 9, 2014
3:53AM

I wish you were here to witness how quickly the night steals away the day. I am sitting on the beach and I am thinking if you. I hope that you are okay. It happened almost as quickly as you stole away my breath. Almost as quickly as you stole away my heart. Night always comes quickly, but it always takes its time to leave...

It has been a week since I have written to you. I needed to get used to this. I needed to. I couldn't spend my life like this. I have not written to you in a while. At least my fingers have not touched my pen and I have not gotten the strength to share my emotions. I have been trying to cover it under the many layers of my skin. But, it hit my inner core and it destroyed tiny bits of it. I have to face the reality that even if I do not write, you haunt me. You have every part of me.

I am wondering if I should give up, but just the thoughts of it makes my body shiver. I feel as if I am worse than a dead person. I am alive. I breathe. I eat. I sleep. I do everything that a normal person does except my emotions are numb. I feel nothing. I kind of do not even exist. I am here physically, but mentally, I have deteriorated. I am a walking skeleton. There are times when body hates you for this. I thought that I would get away from this feeling when I came to Fire Island, but it was impossible. Nothing could take me away from my thoughts. Only you had the power to do such a thing.

God: You told me to read it with my soul and I did. I did this while I was sitting on the beach, next to you, here, in Fire Island. Your eyes tell stories and, sometimes, they are stories that can be translated through silence, just as I communicate to you through silence. It has been your choice to ignore me sometimes, but I have not stopped talking to you even when it seemed like I did. I have not stopped reaching out to you. I haven't left your side. You have never encountered me, but you heard me. At least, that is what I believe. I know that you have heard my words from the pit of your stomach. I know that you have felt me in the pit of your soul, all the way through the corners of your heart and mind. You need to understand that I know that you felt yourself become lost in me again, unknowingly and subconsciously.

I woke up. This was the moment that I believed in God again. He never left.

Letters to Him, 228,

And every single time I breathe,
I hope that God decides to give it to the ocean,
so that the waves steal it away and send it to you, wherever you are.

[M.C.]
August 9, 2014
3:55AM

Letters to Him, 229,

Experience has taught me that silence has revealed more beauty than any word ever could.

[M.C.]
August 9, 2014
3:57AM

Letters to Him, 230,

But, he will be my King in a world full of isolation. And, I did not mind because I did not need another human around me. They caused me to be restless. Every single time I breathed, the rest suffocated me, as if I were inhaling pollution, but he will create gold. He will create meaningful paths out of cracked and dirty cement roads that will lead me to everlasting life... just like God did...You were a God, in my own way...and I worshipped you.

[M.C.]
August 9, 2014
3:59AM

God has a beautiful way of making two souls meet each other. You will not know when, you will not know how, and you will not know where. Only He will possess this information. He is all-powerful. But, in that moment, your life will change, forever. You will feel a type of relief. Before, you were only human: but, now, you have a divine force in you, love. He will exist. I was not certain of much, but I was certain of this.

Letters to Him, 231,

My love is so strong that it destroys the weak hearted. I do not fear that you will come to be weak-hearted because you will understand all the layers of love, just as I have tried to...

[M.C.]
August 10, 2014
3:00AM

Letters to Him, 232,

I do not love you nearly as much as I miss you.

[M.C.]
August 10, 2014
3:13AM

Letters to Him, 233,

I never quite understood. What is a lover without a deep soul? My tears have never touched your skin. I fear that if they did, they would have grown seeds of love that you were incapable of growing. I did not want this love to be one-way.

[M.C.]
August 10, 2014
3:23AM

Letters to Him, 234,

God made her soul a little too black. God made her soul a little too deep. But her eyes were clear and those who took a chance got to see the purity that lived inside of her.

[M.C.]
August 10, 2014
3:33AM

I breathed a little too heavy and my heart was racing. But, that was the only way that she knew it was real. It was tangible. For her, his love was the only thing that existed. And, they all said it. They all said that it was impossible to feel this way. They said that it was too deep. They said that it was too strong. They said that anything strong breaks, doesn't it? It is an ironic concept to invent. But, how about if I found the key? How about if throughout all the chaos, I have found the key to love? How about, if the key that everyone has been searching to find the formula to for so long, was inside of me and I could not see it? I was convinced that his movements kept me alive. He was the fuel to my fire.

Letters to Him, 235,

They asked me why my favorite color was black. All I could think of was this: It is how my soul feels when I think about how mentally far you are from me. It is that empty hole in the universe except my soul feels it twice as worse. It is where I go at 3 AM when I cannot see anything in front of me except the echo of your name in my heart, but you are not within reach.

It is the space between my mind and my heart, the part where they battle constantly, but you are not in sight. It is what I see when I close my eyes, but my heart is a little too tired. It is the color of his lungs when he breathes because he has inhaled a little too much smoke. It is the color of the polluted air at night, when no stars are in sight, so my mind has to come up with your creation alone. It is the color of the 2003 blackout in NYC. Our souls knew each other then, but our bodies have not even met yet. It is the color of dying while my heart is still alive and beating.

It is me without you.

[M.C.]
August 10, 2014
3:43AM

I stared out into the ocean, again. I did not know why I am here. I do not know how I got here. It was as if I was asleep. I do not know where my heart is. I am in the center of the world and I do not know much. I know one thing only. I know that I will love you. And, I don't care if no one understands. The only thing that matters is that I do. It is the only thing that brings me peace in this chaotic mess. I look at the Super moon and I think of you. It is a reminder of how you saved me that night. I will always love you.

Letters to Him, 236,

My soul calls for yours as the waves did that night. I heard them a little too well, that is why u kept echoing inside of me.

[M.C.]
August 10, 2014
3:53AM

Letters to Him, 237,

No other woman could ever love you in such a pure way as I do. My heart has never had any evil intentions, not even for a split second. It has learned you well.

[M.C.]
August 11, 2014
3:00AM

If there was one thing I could tell my younger self, it would probably be this: At times, you will get so disappointed at yourself with how much you will doubt God and you will try to control the outcomes of your life. This will cause you to hate Him at times. But, know this and know it well. Love is not something you will be able to control. Destiny is never something that you will be able to control. What you will be able to do, though, is attract good energy. You will find what you are. You will find what you are looking for as long as you become what you are looking for. It is simple, if you think about it.

Letters to Him, 238,

I kept searching for him in the darkness. I kept hoping that I might find him and he might save me. But, he did not and maybe it was because he was not meant to be my light. I realized that I had been walking backwards with my eyes fixated on one thing that just would not light up instead of walking forward with my eyes open. I was just one look away from missing the flame that led me to a light that would never burn out: you. I am looking forward only.

[M.C.]
August 11, 2014
3:03AM

I walked towards the ocean at 3:00 AM so that I could learn to trust the waves. I closed my eyes as I put both feet in. My mind spoke to me. "Something cut my soul tonight that leaked some words I did not even want to think about. Something cut my eyes tonight that leaked tears that I did not want to expose. Something cut my heart tonight that bled your name all over the papers of writings that I keep in that box. Something cut through my skin tonight, squeezing out every trace of you out of my pores. How I wish something could cut through my mind tonight, but it is the last place where you reside and I will not let go. Don't you get it? You control nothing but your own mind, love."

I started to trust the waves again. **I couldn't control my mind, but my heart started to listen to my mind. It started to learn to compromise.**

Letters to Him, 239,

I always wonder if you will admire me so beautifully even though I might be the main source of your pain. I wonder if you will admire me so beautifully even though I will bluntly define pain's meaning...

[M.C.]
August 11, 2014
3:13AM

Tonight,

I have wanted to become so much like you that I drank and swallowed substances until my vision became blurry and I had forgotten it all: even my very own name. This was your version of living. I became an addict for a night. I wanted to know how you felt when you met pain face to face and why you never thought that you were strong enough to kill it yourself without help from any substance. You failed to realize that your soul had enough power to destroy anything weak. This is how you believed you could overcome it. Tears fly down my cheeks as I write this because even after I follow these steps, I am still drowning in pain. The numbness is present, but my mind still knows how to spell pain well: P-A-I-N.

You never really got rid of your pain, did you? You just covered it up under your skin.

Letters to Him, 240,

And even though you were the definition of pain, I admired you anyway.

[M.C.]
August 11, 2014
3:23AM

I am a pro at talking about pain, aren't I? I know it too well.

Letters to Him, 241,

I will know I have found the one when he cuts through my heart, as if a dagger had touched it, and he feels and tastes the pain that transfers into his body. And, instead of making a bitter face, he will understand it as well as he understands himself.

[M.C.]
August 12, 2014
3:00AM

Letters to Him, 242,

Beauty-
The way his soul loved the ugly,
a little too perfectly.
The way her heart kissed chaos,
a little too silently.

[M.C.]
August 12, 2014
3:03AM

Letters to Him, 243,

Chaos-
I was flying towards you,
and you cut my wings.
I had no direction and
gravity escaped me.

[M.C.]
August 12, 2014
3:13AM

Letters to Him, 244,

But you.

I was weak, to the point where my knees could not hold my limbs together. They were shaken, but you showed me what it was like to be strong yet still.

I was known to write the saddest lines that would crack the hearts of many, but you were the one who made me smile with presence alone.

I was turning quite cold, so cold, that everyone around me thought that I was competing with the bare branches shedding that Fall, but you helped me find the warmth in my soul.

I was as closed as a key to a lover's heart that did not want to shed his secrets to anyone, but you showed me how to open it up, with a key, without me getting any scratches.

I was taught how to breathe again and come alive.

But, you left.

However, it was strange. You did not leave me empty. You left me full.

[M.C.]
August 12, 2014
3:23AM

I kept creating you. You will exist and it will not stop.

Letters to Him, 245,

I called myself selfish.

No one could really get it because, through his or her eyes, my heart was too giving.

They could not understand that in helping them, I was healing myself and placing all of my problems to the side. I had forgotten them.

[M.C.]
August 12, 2014
3:33AM

Letters to Him, 246,

   She looked at everything as if it possessed a deep, meaningful, secret: from the way the rain fell on the ground to the way the goose bumps were able to come alive on one's skin, to noticing smell. She inhaled his scent. They could not help but notice the way that her lips shivered whenever speech, no matter how small, left her body. Her eyes were weapons. They had the ability to see through the deepest souls. Everything she did interrupted the way the universe moved. She knew the meaning of being alive a little too well.

   Nothing was ordinary to her.
   No matter how simple.

[M.C.]
August 13, 2014
3:00AM

I closed my eyes as I kept learning to trust the waves. Something came to my soul suddenly. I ran out and picked up a pen.

Letters to Him, 247 (His Letters to Her),

Everything around me was forever changing. And, I chased it head first, going full speed. My heart was beaten down and bruised, but it was I who inflicted self-harm. I, often wondered, how she was able to remain so stable. She was the definition of constant. I envied how all the ugly could not break her soul yet it could break mine. I couldn't figure out how she was able to remain pure while always around sin. The other women, they all envied the way that she took my breath away by the way she danced around devils while still remaining an angel.

[M.C.]
August 13, 2014
3:02AM

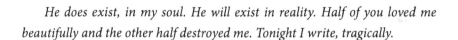

He does exist, in my soul. He will exist in reality. Half of you loved me beautifully and the other half destroyed me. Tonight I write, tragically.

Letters to Him, 248,

He was made up of two people. One half loved me so terribly that he became pure. But, the other half was made up of empty demonic substances that sucked him into his past and destroyed him slowly.

She was made up of one person. She was pure. And, she loved every dusty corner that he was composed of. To her, they had more meaning than anything that was full, fixed, and not broken. But, as she touched his broken glass, trying to fix him, she cut herself to where she eternally bled. She feared that she would never be healed again.

[M.C.]
August 13, 2014
3:03AM

Margaritë Camaj

Letters to Him, 249,

My love was so strong, so unalterable, that I would have followed him to the depths of hell and given up every vision of heaven. But, that was the problem. I willingly gave the fires of hell the power to place a heavy and blinding smoke in front of my vision. And, it almost won the battle against me. I was committed to finding an angel in the soul of the devil. I think it is in that where I found the meaning in love. Never doubt my ability to love evil and transform it into good.

Destructive yet beautiful.

[M.C.]
August 13, 2014
3:13AM

Letters to Him, 250,

Be like the moon,
Hidden in substance
But, lovely when it comes out to play and shows its true colors.

He was the moon,
Hidden inside of me,
But, whenever we connected, it was beautiful.
The chemistry between us that my soul held was undeniable.

[M.C.]
August 13, 2014
3:23AM

Letters to Him, 251,

I think we get lost in our own worlds an awful lot and when we escape them, we notice how small we really are, but how great love really is.

[M.C.]
August 13, 2014
3:33AM

Letters to Him, 252,

The veins that run throughout your body get stronger when you shed tears as the angels from heaven cry their souls out to you. Rainy mornings on the beach are filled with little secrets on how to heal. They are messages that humans come across as cryptic. Nothing is capable of clouding the beauty in pain. It transforms into an infinite superpower if you figure out how it grows from the roots. You are your own kryptonite. I hope you will love yourself as I have grown to love myself...

[M.C.]
August 14, 2014
3:03AM

Letters to Him, 253,

He could be your temporary cure, diluting your vision, blinding your eyesight.
He could be your permanent fix, placing scars on some parts of your skin.
Or, he could be your infinity, finding pieces of your soul no other knew existed,
ones that your own self didn't know.

     The last kind of love is immortal.
     Even death did not know how to defeat it.

[M.C.]
August 15, 2014
3:03AM

He will exist...

Letters to Him, 254,

It was not in me to doubt why I existed.
Your soul became my Creator,
eliminating all sin.
It became so real that my existence came from you.
You became my religion.

You were Godly.

[M.C.]
August 15, 2014
3:13AM

Letters to Him, 255,

There is a place for everyone in dreams,
But how beautiful it would be if we found each other in
reality.

[M.C.]
August 15, 2014
3:23AM

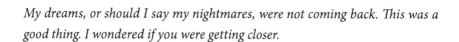

My dreams, or should I say my nightmares, were not coming back. This was a good thing. I wondered if you were getting closer.

Letters to Him, 256,

    I almost told him to take my hand and walk through my mind, but I knew he would make it. He did not even exist in my thoughts.
                    Were you an illusion?

[M.C.]
August 15, 2014
3:33AM

"Shut up Merzi. He will exist."

See, my mind is catching up to my heart.

Letters to Him, 257,

That feeling that you get in the pit of your chest.
That heaviness you feel when you connect with something.
That emptiness yet ease you witness when you are calm.
That comfort you feel when you are in his presence.

That is your soul.

[M.C.]
August 15, 2014
3:43AM

Letters to Him, 258,

You could give me all the space in the atmosphere to breathe, but I have held my breath until my face turned blue. All had led me to turn to you. I no longer suffocate.

You are oxygen.

[M.C.]
August 15, 2014
3:53AM

Letters to Him, 259,

I pray that one day you and I will have battled all of our inner demons and conquered them. I pray that it is in each other that we find the angel of peace.

Hope.

[M.C.]
August 16, 2014
3:13AM

Letters to Him, 260,

He wanted her like hate wanted love.
He wanted her like chaos wanted peace.
He wanted her like God wanted Atheists.
He wanted her like a broken mirror wanted to be fixed.
He wanted her like a dead end road wanted continuance.
He wanted her like empty space wanted meaning.
He wanted her like the weak wanted protection.
He wanted her like the elderly wanted youth.
He wanted her like a cold soul wanted warmth.
He wanted her like sinners wanted purity.

[M.C.]
August 16, 2014
3:23AM

Please, guard your broken heart carefully, for there will be many who will try to get in between the cracks and fill it with poison...only to run away and steal the pieces. I have learned the levels of love and of myself almost thoroughly up until this present moment...I grow daily...

Letters to Him, 261,

It was strange. I was trying to fill this void for quite a while now. Then, you arrived, so gently, but so tempting. With a simple hello, my void was filled. Something that I still couldn't figure out. You could.

Within seconds. Timeless.

[M.C.]
August 16, 2014
3:33AM

Letters to Him, 262,

Her world was composed of only him and her because the power of his soul killed off all of the others. This was love's version of the survival of the fittest.

[M.C.]
August 16, 2014
3:43AM

Letters to Him, 263,

She looked at anything that was dying as if it could come alive. She looked at it as if she could resuscitate it, give it oxygen, or make a heartbeat survive. Some called her hope. He called her life.

[M.C.]
August 16, 2014
3:53AM

Letters to Him, 264,

In the dark, you come to me and I come to you, so pure, completely by chance. Like a thief, you steal my reality. Like the devil, you capture my soul, so effortlessly. I am unsure if this is good, but it is happiness. All perception is lost.

[M.C.]
August 17, 2014
3:00AM

...and just like that, I was lost. I couldn't write anymore. I don't know how, but these letters have escaped me.

I almost feel as if I loved something that was nonexistent. Do you know how fucking scary and draining this is? Do you know that my heart has become so cold that not even the strongest flame of fire could have burned it—or made it warmer? It is now almost the end of August and I feel colder than ever. You are not in my presence. I had bursts of you throughout this year, but it was all through words, okay? It has been one fucking year and although I have grown, my heart has remained constant and the same. I wanted you to either come or for me to have eliminated you of me—but what a tragedy the elimination of you from me would be!

Sometimes, I hate myself for it because I think that I am not strong enough to overcome you. Other times, I praise and love myself for it because it is what keeps me alive. You are what kept me breathing to this very day, whether I want to acknowledge it or not. And, that is why I say that I am strong because someone weak would not be able to bare all of these emotions. They would have let you go a long time ago. They would have let love go a long time ago. Me, on the other hand, kept holding on to something that I wasn't even sure would actually exist. That is what they would all say. But me, I would say that my soul believed that you would exist. And, how did I do this? All because I fell in love with you through my mind.

I don't understand it. And, do you want to know something else? Sometimes, that feeling faintly…it…it disappears. Like now, these letters have to come to an end because I have given my all to these letters and they have almost eaten me alive. How ironic is it that you were my soul, but you have almost taken it away from me. I have almost become just pen and paper. You know that they say to not sell your soul to the devil, and I am trying not to. You are not the devil—that is not what I am saying. You know, don't get me wrong because even if you were the devil, I would probably still love you anyway, because that is how unconditional my love is. You are my soul mate. No one before you mattered and I fear that no one after you will be able to take your place.

These words have swallowed me up into something that is so unrecognizable. It is as if I do not even recognize myself. And, I do not get it because I literally isolated myself from everything and tried to figure myself out, but my mind almost took control of me--fully. I still look at the water, often, and instead of seeing my reflection, I see your face. No, fuck that! I see your soul. That is why I go back to the water every now and then, and that is why I am often blinded.

You have become my mirror, but I barely even see myself anymore. I see us. I have transformed into you. I believe that God intended for this to happen. I am not an angel and I have never claimed to be one. I have more flaws than anyone could ever see. And you, although many may have differed, you are not evil. You have so many sins that you carry proudly, but my soul has chosen to overlook them because I see something in you. You never had evil intentions. God wanted the angel to meet the devil, but could the two ever survive? I always try to go back to that moment and think about if this was ever possible or did I just repeatedly practice these thoughts in my head like a song that you could never forget, like the waves of the ocean that beautifully crash into the shore. Or, to my tragedy, was this just an illusion? Could I never find you because you were never there? Maybe. This is possible. And if we shall never be together, I am certain that our souls will, somehow, be one anyway. We are infinite. I still believe that he will exist even if it will take a while for him to arrive.

Last Letter to Him...

I do not have much else to say except that whatever I say comes from my soul. I was never a good speaker. Forgive me. I think it is partially because I have so many conflicting situations occurring in my head at the same time. They battle, constantly, so when I say something, it is a tiny piece of one big puzzle that even I can't figure out. It fucks with my mental on a daily basis.

But, I thank you, for reading my letters over this past year. You went through everything with me, by my side, and now you know some of the emotions that are inside of me. Hopefully, now you get to understand a tiny piece of me. I know that when these letters end, we might never meet. We might never know each other, partially due to the flaws of our very own humanity.

But, thank you for understanding—or trying to understand—how I love through these writings. At least we were able to transfer love to each other through writings that you might one day find. Love is pain. I firmly believe that. But, I also believe that love has the power to heal. Love is a contradiction, just like I am. At least we gave each other peace for a little bit of time. Or, maybe, I have given myself peace. I might never be able to share this again with anyone, but we have become each other. Isn't that beautiful? We have each other in us, spiritually. That is enough. This is not my wish. I wish it were guaranteed that we will meet.

Maybe in this life or maybe in the next. But, this is destiny. And if destiny believes in us, as much as I do, he will exist.

I have been to every little part of my mind and I have learned myself fully. The corners of my mind are not so dusty anymore. I am ready for you. I wandered everywhere until I knew myself well. In turn, I knew you. He will exist.

P.S. He will exist. Another woman can capture his eyes, but I have captured his soul. He is forever altered. He will be changed because of me. No matter how small, the world thinks it is, I reside in his soul and I have allowed it to suffocate me, through no one's fault but my own. But how could I deny my soul's home? I couldn't. You all have no right to judge me. I belonged here, no matter how short my time was cut. It was where I was meant to live during this time. I have lived for you. You were my beautiful tragedy. I leave these letters here.

Turn the page...

Have you come back to find me? Have these letters ended up in your hands? Have you read this until the end? If you have come back to find me, wherever the path has lead me, wherever I may be, I hope that you have learned my secrets and you at least know. I hope you learn that my love for you is so strong that death does not stand a chance. Please look for me. Please do not let me go. I hope that you have fallen in love with my mind, my heart, and my soul no matter how damaging they can be. And, if anyone else has found these letters on Fire Island, no matter the time, I hope you have learned at least one thing: fight. Fight for your heart, fight for your mind, and fight for your soul. Let no one alter it. In doing so, you love yourself and you will win. If not in this life, I promise that God has reserved a place for us. We all have one person in our past that destroys us and breaks us into pieces, and these pieces have turned into words, but these words are for you. They made me feel alive again no matter how dead they thought that I was.

Have you found me? Have you cared to know that this is my hiding space because no one before you would have even cared to analyze and know that about me? But you, you have memorized my movements…here in Fire Island. He will exist. Until next time.

Printed in the United States
By Bookmasters